A SHOT AT MERCY

A Shot

At

Mercy

Timothy R. Baldwin

INDIES UNITED PUBLISHING HOUSE, LLC

Second Edition published January 2021
By Indies United Publishing House, LLC

First edition published 2019 under *Bloodshot*

Cover art designed by
Timothy R. Baldwin and Harry Carpenter

ISBN: 978-1-64456-229-1 (paperback)
ISBN: 978-1-64456-230-7(mobi)
ISBN: 978-1-64456-231-4 (ePub)

Library of Congress Control Number: 2020951697

INDIES UNITED PUBLISHING HOUSE, LLC
P.O. BOX 3071
QUINCY, IL 62305-3071
www.indiesunited.net

Also by Timothy R. Baldwin

A Kahale and Claude Mystery Series

Book 1: Camp Lenape (2019)
Book 2: Shadows of Doubt (2020)
Book 2.5: A Bazaar Christmas (2020)
Book 3: Operation Varsity Blues (2020)

These and more at
https://www.indiesunited.net/timothy-baldwin

PROLOGUE

It is late Fall, and the chill of winter has already set in. This chill seems to seep within Emmitt's soul as he listens to the sounds around him. In a distant corridor, an alarm buzzes, and the metallic opening of a door clangs and echoes off the concrete walls.

"Prisoner entering!"

Shifting uncomfortably in a faded plastic seat, Emmitt stares through the plexiglass window serving as a barrier between himself and another world. Others sat here before him, and others will sit here after him. He offers up a silent prayer for mercy and healing, for the strangers who will occupy this seat, and for the ones they love.

Another door slams shut, and Emmitt looks up. His daughter, Lindsay Jane, enters. Though her blonde hair appears disheveled, she looks better than the last time he saw her. Her blue eyes, once veiny, are clear. Her skin appears to sag where it should be taut and youthful, especially for a twenty-two-year-old like herself. He wants to embrace his daughter and heal her unseen wounds – years of neglect on his part and years of addiction on her part. Many times, he tried but failed to

1

keep her from the same path he walked.

Sighing heavily, she sits. They smile weakly at each other and pick up their receivers.

"Hey, daddy," Lindsay says.

"Hey, princess," he whimpers as he chokes back tears.

They share a moment of silence. As with such moments, they both think the same thing: *How the hell did we get to this point?*

CHAPTER ONE

January 30, 1994

Machinery buzzes with life, and Emmitt Wasson still beams with pride at his daughter Lindsay Jane's baptism early that morning. He would've stayed for the pot lock afterward, but work called needing volunteers for overtime. With a few months on the job and in desperate need of extra income and experience, Emmitt jumped at the opportunity.

Tonight, he oversees the conveyor belt where he monitors cases of soda boxed and tied upon shipping pallets.

A great hand clasps Emmitt on the shoulder. The bass of the bearded giant, Leo Andreadis, booms above the noise.

"Congratulations, my friend!"

Catching sourness to Leo's breath, Emmitt turns his attention back on the conveyor.

Leo rests an arm on the safety railing. "I would've stuck around after your daughter's baptism, but something came up."

"I appreciate you coming," Emmitt says. "So, you're a

member at St. Andrews?"

"Not exactly," Leo says. "But I take my son when he's in town."

"Oh, okay." Emmitt turns his full attention on Leo. "How old is your son?"

Leo averts his eyes. "Troy, my son is three."

Emmitt swallows. "How are you and his mother?"

"Divorced," Leo says in barely a whisper.

As Emmitt forms a question, a sudden crash comes from the conveyor belt. Leo slams down the emergency button, bringing the warehouse and the conversation to a halt.

"Looks like we've got a mess to clean up," Leo says. He turns, and Emmitt follows him off the platform. Once on the warehouse floor, they find exploded bottles and pools of soda surrounding the pallet lift.

"Let's start here," Leo says. "I'll go find a pail and a mop while you clean up some of those bottles."

While Leo runs off, Emmitt climbs beneath the pallet lift and begins to clear away some of the debris. While there, the convey clangs to life, and the lift begins to drop.

Emmitt pivots, calling out. "Shut that off!"

With little room between himself and the moving machinery parts, he dashes for safety. As he ducks, he slips. The weight of the lift bears down upon him. For a flashing moment, scenes from the morning's baptismal service come to mind.

His wife, Maggie, hold their baby Lindsay Jane in her arms. Emmitt makes the sign of the cross on the baby's forehead. Father Klein is claiming their daughter for Christ. Emmitt is vowing to raise her in the faith.

Emmitt grits his teeth. "Get this fucking thing off me!"

Footsteps clamor down the metal planks.

"Holy shit, Em!" Leo calls. "Hold tight, my friend."

Leo clamors up the steps, calling "Joe!"

"Hey, who turned the machinery off?" Joe shouts.

"Forget about that," Emmitt blurts. "I'm caught under

the lift!"

Wide-eyed, Joe appears. "Leo's called for help... but..."

When Joe's voice trails off, Emmitt attempts to catch a glimpse of the damage. He gives up as he cries out in pain.

Joe kneels. "Emmitt, just sit tight and don't move."

"Easy for you to say," Emmitt says. "Didn't you see the safety lock?"

"It wasn't on, so —"

"He's down here," Leo calls out, cutting Joe's explanation short.

* * *

Once at the hospital, the doctor immediately sees Emmitt and orders an X-Ray and an MRI. When Maggie and family friends Frank and Daniella arrive, they wait to hear Emmitt's condition. The doctor assures them Emmitt will indeed walk again. But he will always limp and experience some pain, which he will be able to manage through medication.

When the doctor leaves, Maggie gives Emmitt a weak smile. She cradles baby Lindsay Jane, who sleeps soundly in her arms.

"We're going to be okay," Maggie whispers.

Emmitt nods and refuses to voice his dismay and anger at his coworkers' carelessness.

"Emmitt, we're here for you," says Frank, placing an arm around Daniella. "We're here for you, Maggie, and Lindsay, just like we were here for you through A.A."

"Thanks, Frank," Emmitt says. Before he can recall those dark, painful years prior to his marriage, Emmitt squelches the thoughts.

He can't help but think about his predicament. Over the years, he has never sustained any severe injuries, not even during his active duty overseas in combat zones. Not once has he been shot or suffered from paralysis. But now, with both legs crushed and moments before surgery, Emmitt lies silent in his hospital bed. He holds a stoic expression as he casts a shadowy accusation upon the only man who could have screwed this up — Leo Andreadis.

Chapter Two

August 15, 1994

"You are going to work," Maggie states firmly. Emmitt hangs up the phone.

It is mid-August. The couple sits in the living room. Emmitt still holds the phone in his lap.

"Babe," Emmitt says as he stands and winces. He flexes one leg and another. "I shouldn't have to. The lawyer said we'll get two-hundred-and-fifty grand! And that's after the court and medical fees. So, with this money coming in—"

"It wasn't a question," Maggie interrupts. "That money will run out. And, you know yourself. You'll grow restless, and I'll get annoyed with you around all the time with nothing to do."

Emmitt, knowing that she speaks the truth, frowns and nods as he reaches into his pocket. In his hand, he rolls around a small pill bottle, remnants of his doctor's prescription for pain medication. He's already taken one just a few hours ago, but his doctor said to take them as often as needed. Making a mental note to renew this prescription, he takes it out, opens the bottle, and pops a pill in his mouth.

"Is your leg hurting you?" Maggie asks.

"I'm okay," replies Emmitt. "Just a sudden sharp stiff pain when I stood."

"When's the last time you did the stretches your physical therapist told you to do?"

Emmitt sighs. "This morning."

"Well, maybe you need to get it checked out. We can call and make an appointment now." She stands and reaches to take the phone from Emmitt.

"It's okay," Emmitt says as he pulls the phone away from her. "I think it's going away. Just gotta walk it off."

"Or medicate it off," Maggie says. "You know, you need a hobby, or a job, or both. Hey, maybe you can start to put that rifle you keep locked up in the mantle to use. When's the last time you've been hunting with Frank?"

"Too long. Not since before Lindsay was born. Don't worry, though Once I can really move, Frank and I'll go hunting again."

Maggie narrows her eyes and crosses her arms. "What'll you do in the meantime?"

"I'll spend time with Lindsay. I was reading a magazine that mentioned girls her age really benefit from having a father around."

"And their mothers," Maggie replies sharply. She walks toward the living room, then turns to Emmitt before she leaves. "Maybe I'll get a hobby or some work. Maybe something artsy, like at one of those stores where they frame pictures."

"Maybe," Emmitt says, closing the distance between himself and Maggie. "But you don't have to get work. Not right now, anyway. I'll look for something when I'm cleared for work."

At these words, Maggie tightens her lips and nods slowly. "Okay. Well, I'm going to look anyway. Maybe we'll both get something. Wouldn't that be great?" Maggie forces a smile.

"Yeah." Emmitt pauses. "Maybe it would be."

Maybe feels like a void between Emmitt and Maggie.

Maybe survives on the pretense of an absolute that doesn't exist. Not unless Emmitt and Maggie believe in endless potential and courage – a necessity for anyone, who would undertake the duty of raising a child in the faith, free of forgotten *maybes*.

CHAPTER THREE

June 16, 1997

Early one Sunday morning, Emmitt's sleep-in is interrupted when the bed shakes. Next to him, he feels the weight of the bed redistribute as Maggie climbs. Her bare feet patter on hardwood floors as she makes her way toward the bathroom. Rolling over, Emmitt catches her eyes as she turns to close the door behind her.

"Is everything okay?" he asks.

"Just some lower back pain," says Maggie from the bathroom. "I'll be all right."

"Take some of my pain meds. I should have some in the medicine cabinet."

Maggie nods as she closes the bathroom door, creating a barrier between herself and Emmitt. The cry of Lindsay Jane, who is now three years old, stirs him from the bed. Sitting up and placing his feet upon the cool floor, Emmitt scowls as he looks at the clock, which now reads seven minutes after five o'clock in the morning.

Bemoaning the loss of sleep, Emmitt follows his daughter's voice. Her cry turns into a piercing scream. He stands and takes one short, limping stride after another until the joints in his legs loosen and the pain and stiffness subside enough for him to walk with a little more ease. Finally, he comes to his daughter's room. A warm glow from the room's night-light spills into the hallway where he stands and waits. Lindsay's cries subside until they are a quiet whimper. Emmitt picks her up and pulls her close. As he does this, he feels the warm but dry pull-up, which she now wears only at night.

"Do you need to go potty?" he asks.

Lindsay nods, and he follows her to the hallway bathroom and waits by the door until she is ready for him to help her clean up. After this, they go to the bedroom to find Maggie sitting on the end of the bed. As they enter, she gives them both a weary smile.

"Lindsay Jane, don't you have something to tell your papa?" asks Maggie. When Lindsay shakes her head, Maggie crosses her arms. "Well, we're waiting."

"Okay, mama," Lindsay obediently answers. She turns to Emmitt. "Happy Father's Day, papa!" Lindsay reaches her arms up to Emmitt, who lifts her up.

"Thank you, princess," he says. As he rocks Lindsay in his arms, he gazes at Maggie.

Maggie nods and smiles weakly. He can see that there is clearly something wrong.

"Papa," Lindsay says. "I wanna go play."

"Oh, princess," Emmitt says as he places Lindsay down. "It's too early to play. Why don't you head back to bed, and I promise we'll do something fun after church today?"

"Okay, papa." Once on the floor, Lindsay darts away. Her tiny feet slapping upon the hallway floor can be heard until she turns into her bedroom.

"Are you sure you're all right?" Emmitt asks.

"I'll be okay," replies Maggie. "I just need to stretch and do some yoga. Not to mention, we've got church and Father's Day brunch." She waves Emmitt away. "Don't worry about me."

Knowing his wife, Emmitt decides against arguing

about her point, which she has already made, or a point she refuses to address. He turns down the hallway to get Lindsay ready for church. While he's gone, Maggie stretches in the master bedroom and gets ready.

An hour later, after everyone has washed, Maggie assures Emmitt the hot shower has relieved her aches.

* * *

At church, Father Klein gives the homily on the following words of scripture: "If anyone wishes to come after me, he must deny himself and take up his cross daily and follow me."

As Father Klein speaks, Emmitt re-reads these words, self-denial, and the image of a cross play at his conscience. He recalls Leo, a man he hasn't communicated with in years. Though Leo is the one ultimately responsible for his injuries, Emmitt holds the choice to give meaning to his pain. Emmitt also realizes he has a choice to return to work, even if it is a part-time gig, like what Maggie has mentioned. Only that his gig wouldn't be artsy. Maybe it would have something to do with tools or hunting.

Glancing up, he sees that Maggie has been gazing at him. Her blue eyes soften. As the two make eye contact, they embrace. Emmitt kisses Maggie on the lips, but Lindsay impatiently squirms between them.

"I gotta go potty," Lindsay says loud enough to send her voice bouncing off the high ceilings of the church. A few parishioners chuckle in response while others glare at the couple. Emmitt is sure the latter wonder why he seems incapable of keeping his daughter quiet.

"I'll take her," Emmitt whispers. He stands and takes Lindsay by the hand.

Once in the narthex of the church, he spots Leo Andreadis down the hallway. There are several single-use bathrooms where he stands. Emmitt assumes Leo waits outside one of the bathrooms for his son. Leo spots him and waves. Emmitt gives him a quick wave back, then turns quickly down an adjacent hallway leading to the family room. While Lindsay, who has insisted she is a big girl that can take care of herself, is alone in the bathroom, Emmitt waits outside. He bows his head, knowing that he must also make amends with his former coworker. For his suffering to have any meaning, he must forgive Leo, the cause of this suffering. He glances up the hallway and sighs. He expects to see Leo, but the man is no longer there.

A flush from the toilet within the bathroom interrupts his thoughts, and Lindsay opens the door.

"I can't reach the sink," she says.

Emmitt follows her into the bathroom. At the sink, he runs the water, waiting for it to warm up. He places one hand beneath the running water to test the temperature and uses the other hand to adjust the sink knob accordingly. Once the water feels suitable for Lindsay, he lifts her up to help wash her hands. Adding soap to their hands, together the two sing "Happy Birthday" while washing their hands for at least 20 seconds. Emmitt prides himself with instilling the right values, like good hygiene and proper manners, in his daughter. He wants to be the best father he can be for Lindsay.

Once their hands are dry, Emmitt and Lindsay are ready to rejoin the congregation. Lindsay charges to the end of the hallway and stops. She waits for Emmitt to catch up, so she can walk with him as father and daughter. When they return to their pew to finish service, they sit by Maggie, shifting her weight in her spot. She smiles at Emmitt, and the family sits quietly until the service ends. From there, they head to IHOP.

As expected, the line to IHOP is long, but Emmitt doesn't mind. Father's Day brunch after church has become the Wasson family tradition these past three years. Seeing no point in breaking the tradition now, Emmitt pulls into a parking lot so crowded it could rival any pre-game tailgate party he has ever attended.

Yet, as he drives through the parking lot for a free space, he glances beside him at Maggie. She squirms in her seat.

"Is your back bothering you again?" he asks.

"Yeah," she says and adds a smile, tight and narrow so that her lips become pale as they pull into her mouth. "I don't know if it is worse or better."

Emmitt frowns. "It seems worse than this morning. Maybe we should—"

"No, there's a spot," Maggie says forcibly. She points beyond him, so that Emmitt must look ahead.

Seeing another car around the lane, Emmitt punches the gas and puts on his blinker. He pulls in and turns to block the other vehicle from taking the spot. The driver in the other vehicle honks and flashes his light. Emmitt waves at the driver and throws the van into reverse. He backs into the parking space and looks straight ahead as he waits for the other car to pass.

"You know," Emmitt says, "maybe we should get you to a hospital."

When Maggie doesn't reply, he diverts his attention from the parking lot and looks at her. He sees that the vanity mirror is down, and Maggie is repeatedly opening and closing her mouth. She does this a few times before she realizes that Emmitt is looking at her.

"Sorry," she says as she closes the mirror. "I'm okay. I just have this ache in my jaw, like I chewed gum for several hours nonstop."

"That's not good," Emmitt says. "Between your back and jaw, maybe we should get it checked out." He shifts the car into reverse.

Maggie places her hand upon Emmitt's. "I'll get it checked out tomorrow, okay? And look, the other driver is driving off."

But Emmitt doesn't look. Instead, his attention is on Maggie until a yawn from the backseat diverts his gaze to where Lindsay is waking up.

"Where are we?" she asks.

"IHOP, honey," Maggie says. "You ready for some pancakes?" Lindsay nods, which makes Maggie smile.

As Maggie gets out of the car, Emmitt notices how stiff she seems, like someone in great pain. He lifts Lindsay from her car seat and sets her on the ground.

"Can Papa carry me?" Lindsay asks.

Mechanically, he lifts Lindsay up. And with Maggie's arm around his waist and his daughter on his shoulders, they join the long line of hungry fathers with their families.

As they wait, Emmitt sees that Maggie is massaging her lower back with both hands while she slowly takes deep breaths. From behind Emmitt, an elderly woman taps him on the back.

"Sir," she says, "I think your wife is having a heart attack."

* * *

In the hospital waiting room, Emmitt stands a few paces away from the chair where Lindsay sits and hugs her doll. Beside her sits Daniella and Frank. Emmitt begins to pace. Frank stands and places a hand on his shoulder.

"You should sit down," Frank says. "It's only been a half hour since the surgery's started."

"Doc said it should only take a half hour," Emmitt grumbles.

"It's not likely they started right away," Frank says. "Sit with me."

Emmitt turns away and crosses his arms. He stares at the television mounted in the corner wall of the waiting room. Its silent screen airs some news station broadcasting the weather. Closed captioning scrolls one choppy, unread sentence after the next as Emmitt looks on. Someone tugs at his shirt hanging loosely by his waist. He glances down where Lindsay stands by him.

"Is Mommy going to be okay?" Lindsay asks. Her wide blue eyes reflect the light of the fluorescent bulbs humming from the ceiling. As Lindsay waits for a response from her father, she clutches her doll even tighter with both arms.

Emmitt squats and takes Lindsay in his arms. As he does, she releases one arm from her doll to give her dad a hug.

"Let's say a prayer for Mommy, okay?" Emmitt asks. Lindsay closes her eyes, and Emmitt begins to pray. "Jesus..." he pauses as tears well up in his eyes. He clears his throat and continues, "Please be with Mommy and the doctors. Amen."

"Amen," Lindsay says. "Can we sit down now?"

With his daughter still in his arms, Emmitt sits between Frank and Daniella.

"Hang in there, bud," Frank says.

In the waiting room, time passes slowly, especially for Emmitt and his party. While they wait, doctors and nurses are paged over the intercom, and the rest of the hospital staff dressed in pale green push patients garbed in white in gurneys and wheelchairs. But Emmitt and his party hardly pay attention to the mundane activities in the hospital. Finally, two staff members emerge from a set of double doors. The doctor, a greying haired man whom Emmitt met hours before, ambles toward Emmitt. Just a few paces behind him, the surgical assistant follows. Emmitt stands and waits as they approach slowly. The doctor smiles, but Emmitt fears the worst.

"Mr. Wasson, your wife's in recovery," says the doctor. "She had a narrow artery, which we used a stent to open. She'll recover very soon. It's a good thing you all caught it when you did."

"Thank you," Emmitt whispers. He exhales the breath he had been holding and sits.

"When she is awake," replies the surgical assistant, "a nurse will come to get you."

The doctor and surgical assistant leave, so they can resume their work beyond the double doors.

Whether a half hour or an hour passes, Emmitt does

not know. He is only thankful when a nurse appears to take him and his party to see his wife. In the room, Frank and Daniella stand back as Emmitt approaches Maggie's bed. Although she lies drugged up and surgery worn, Emmitt thinks she is still beautiful. His eyes glisten with tenderness as he takes her hand in his. Then, he leans in and kisses her on the forehead.

"I have to go," he whispers. "But we'll be back." After a few more minutes, Emmitt and the others leave.

* * *

Alone in the quiet of the night, Emmitt sits on the couch. The drive home gave him time to clear his head. Lindsay has long since gone to sleep. There is a knock at the door, which startles him since it is eleven o'clock at night. Another knock comes more rapidly.

"Emmitt, open the door," says a muffled, familiar voice on the other end. "It's me, Leo."

Emmitt remains seated and hopes his unwanted guest will leave. When the knock becomes even more persistent, Emmitt stands with a huff. He flicks on the light-switch and opens the door. In the pale, white glow of the porch light, Leo Andreadis flashes Emmitt a weak smile.

"I'm sorry to hear about your wife," he says. He holds up a six-pack of beer. "Mind if I come in?"

"I do," Emmitt says.

With the screen door between himself and Leo, Emmitt is a stony sentinel frowning at the man he once would have considered a work friend. Yet in that stance, the day's near tragedy washes over the old wounds of suffering incurred as a result of Leo's carelessness. Before him, Leo slouches with a droopy arm holding a six-pack. Like the man holding it, the cardboard casing is beginning to sag, dripping small beads of condensation upon the porch as it soaks in the thin layer of moisture collecting on each exposed can.

"Let's sit on the porch," Emmitt replies. "Lindsay's asleep. Don't want to wake her."

As Emmitt opens the door, Leo draws himself up and follows Emmitt to the wicker furniture where the two men sit. Leo pops open a beer and offers it to Emmitt, which he refuses with a wave of his hand.

"Had to take some pain meds today for the legs," he says.

"Shit," Leo says. He gulps his beer and wipes his mouth. "Saw you in church today."

Emmitt nods curtly as Leo takes another swig. "Was your son with you?"

"Yeah, but he's back with his mom now," Leo says.

On the porch, the two men simply look at each other. Mothers flutter between them toward the light. Leo guzzles his beer and wipes his mouth on his sleeve. Finally, Leo clanks an empty can upon the table between them.

"I'm really sorry," Leo says. "I know this is a bad time and all, but I thought I'd come to talk to you about the accident."

Emmitt clenches his jaws and sucks in a breath. As heat inflames his chest and washes over his face, his attention is drawn once again to his legs.

"You're right, Leo," Emmitt says. "Now is definitely a bad time. It's been three years. Why now?"

Leo shrugs. "I guess no time is really a good time." He pops another can open and takes a drink.

Though an apology or excuse is almost always on the horizon of a lengthy and often lame explanation, Emmitt stands and decides that he need not wait for either one.

"Look, Leo," Emmitt says. "I forgive you."

"That means a lot," Leo says. He clears his throat. "But I still need to tell you something."

Emmitt sits. Leo, a man who once stood tall, confident, and boisterous, seems to sag deeper into his seat.

"On the day of the accident, I wasn't quite right," says Leo. "I'd been drinking." He sighs. "Actually, I'm always drunk."

At hearing Leo's confession, Emmitt thinks back to that day. Nothing about Leo's behavior that day, sour breath aside, would've indicated drunkenness.

"Hey," Emmitt says, "I've been where you are, and I want to help."

Before him, Leo Andreadis crumples under the burden which Emmitt supposes Leo has carried long before the accident. Emmitt stands and offers Leo his hand. Leo takes Emmitt's hand and pulls him into an embrace.

"Confession leads to healing, my friend," says Emmitt. "I'll help you through this."

Chapter Four

December 25, 1999

Emmitt awakes. Sitting up, he attempts to rub out the blur of a partial night's sleep from his eyes. Unable to do so, he turns to the digital clock on the nightstand. He squints and tries to read the glowing red numerical display blinking rapidly as if the power had gone out during the night. Turning from the clock, he stares into the darkness of the room until his eyes adjust to the moon's light gleaming gently through metallic blinds and casting horizontal lines of light upon the bedroom wall.

As he waits in bed, he listens to Maggie's gentle snoring. He smiles with gratitude. It's been three years since her heart surgery, and Emmitt is thankful she's still here. While Maggie's health seems stable, Emmitt's legs have hardly improved since his post-accident physical therapy.

Emmitt spent half the night listening to Maggie snoring and the other half of the night focusing on throbbing pain in his legs. With blurred eyes barely adjusted to the limited light, dizziness and unbearable pain struck his right leg. Beside him, Maggie lets out a soft groan as she rolls over. When she has finished rolling over, he feels the warmth of her palm upon his back.

"What time is it, Em?" she asks softly.

"It should be two-thirty in the morning," he says with a yawn. "I think the power went out earlier."

"Must've been the snowstorm," Maggie says as she rolls over.

He answers her with a grunt as he rubs his eyes and lifts his right leg to massage out the pain. As he does so, he winces.

"Here," Maggie says as she sits up. "Scoot over here and let me help you with that."

As he shifts his weight, Emmitt's head starts to spin. His stomach begins to churn. He swallows and sends the sickening sensation back down.

"Does your leg hurt a lot?" Maggie asks when she sees him wince.

"No, it's not my leg," groans Emmitt. "It's the stomach."

Forgetting the pain in his leg, he scoots out of bed and pivots to the bathroom. He flips on the light, shuts the door, and kneels at the toilet. After a few dry heaves, Emmitt hurls. His stomach releases its grip on last night's dinner with violent, rapid splashes of vomit into the toilet. When finished, he stands and turns on the faucet until it runs warm water. He cups water into his hands, splashes his face, and takes a sip. He swishes, rinses, and spits out the water until the sour taste in his mouth is gone. Once finished, he turns the faucet off, flushes the toilet, and dries his hands and face. Then, he silently stands in front of the mirror, not seeing himself but the medicine cabinet behind the glass.

Hidden within the medicine cabinet is a bottle of pills beckoning to him. He cannot recall his last dosage.

It must've been a few days. No, a few hours since I had some, he thinks.

Emmitt reaches his hand out toward the sliding glass door and stops himself. He glances at the bathroom, locks it, and then turns the faucet on again.

Sliding the mirrored cabinet door to the right, he sees a pharmaceutical assortment of Maggie's antiaging creams and other beauty supplies. None of these products can fulfill his immediate need. Someone knocks on the door.

"Em, are you all right?" asks Maggie. She jiggles the door handle. "Why's the door locked?"

"Sorry, I must've locked it accidentally," he lies.

"Do you need any help?" Maggie's voice sounds more urgent.

A moment's hesitation passes over him. "I'll be out in a minute." When Maggie doesn't respond, his heart races.

All I need to do is take one more pill, and the pain will be gone, he reasons.

When Emmitt hears Maggie shuffle from the door, he removes bottles and canisters, placing each on the sink and toilet lid. Once the cabinet is clear, he removes a rear panel of the cabinet. On a makeshift shelf within the hollow of the exposed wall sits a single translucent orange bottle. Emmitt considers if he should consume the content of this bottle as the steady stream of the faucet continues to swirl down the drain. He shakes his head.

Taking the bottle in his hand, he shakes it and smiles. The familiar rattle of the pills inside comforts him, so he opens the bottle with a push and a twist. He dumps one pill in his hand and pops it into his mouth, holding the pill there on his tongue and savoring its bitter taste. He closes the lid of the bottle, which he returns to the safety of the hollow in the wall. After cupping his hands under the running water, he washes the pill down in one gulp. Mechanically, he knocks the panel back into the wall and returns each bottle and canister to its rightful place on the cabinet shelves.

Maggie will never know, he thinks.

After shutting off the water, Emmitt unlocks the door and opens it. Maggie leaps up from the bed and embraces him.

"I was so worried," she says with tears in her voice.

"Hey," Emmitt says as he lifts her chin to look into her eyes. "I'm okay."

"Then, why?" She pulls back without releasing him. "Why were you in there so long?"

"Just cleaning up."

In the darkness of the night, Maggie's face tightens. She doesn't push Emmitt for more answers. She simply turns away.

"Let's go back to bed," he says. "Lindsay will be up in a few hours."

"Yeah," Maggie says with a shaky laugh as she pulls the covers over her. "It's Christmas."

Joining her side, Emmitt leans into his wife, kissing her on the cheek. "Merry Christmas."

She greets his lips with her own. Contained within that kiss are years of passion, pain, and struggle made sweet with the love they have for each other.

* * *

Emmitt hears the faint jingling of Christmas bells as he turns over in bed and pulls the covers over his head. The jingling grows louder and livelier until it ends with the weight of six-year-old Lindsay Jane plopping beside him in bed. He figures she must've entered the bedroom while he was in the bathroom. With another jingle or two, she shifts her weight and hugs Emmitt.

"Merry Christmas, Daddy," Lindsay whispers.

Though his eyes are closed, and his head is still covered by the blankets over his head, Emmitt feels the warmth of her breath within less than an inch of his face.

"Merry Christmas," he says cheerfully. "Where's your mother?"

"Making waffles." Lindsay gets up and pounces on her dad's chest.

"Okay, well it seems like it's time for breakfast." Emmitt slowly sits up. "Shall we go down?"

"Uh-huh."

Emmitt peels off the covers along with Lindsay, lifting her into his arms. In the holiday spirit, he wraps her in the covers and swaddles her, like baby Jesus.

"Daddy," Lindsay giggles. "You got me all stuck."

"Well," he says, "I guess you'll just have to eat breakfast like that."

He stretches and throws on a t-shirt before he throws Lindsay over his shoulder and carries her downstairs. On the way down, her squirming and giggling loosen the blankets. The blankets hang like drapes over Emmitt's shoulders, creating a tripping hazard. After setting Lindsay down, he tosses the blankets in a wad on the bottom two steps. With Lindsay leading the way, Emmitt follows her into the kitchen.

"Merry Christmas, Emmitt," Maggie says as she stands to exchange a ritualistic morning kiss, after which she steps away with wide eyes and furrowed brow. "How'd you sleep?"

"Better," Emmitt says. He surveys the kitchen table stacked with all kinds of food: waffles with maple syrup, scrambled eggs, and two steaming cups of coffee. "This all looks really great."

As the family of three sits down, there is a knock at the door, which opens before an answer. Getting up from the table, Emmitt exits the kitchen and enters the foyer where he meets Maggie's parents.

"Merry Christmas, Emmitt," Willis says. His voice is loud and gruff like a large dog barking. Willis offers Emmitt a firm handshake and pulls him into a two-armed embrace.

Meanwhile, Lindsay's ornamented stocking feet jingle as she runs to join them in the foyer. Pulling away from Willis, Emmitt is sure his daughter will be asking for

Gramma and Grampa. Maggie follows behind Lindsay and takes her parents' belongings. Emmitt turns to Claire, his mother-in-law. She is a soft-spoken, petite woman, he embraces, exchanging with her a dry kiss on the cheek.

"We were just about getting ready to sit down for breakfast," Emmitt says. "We thought you'd be here much later. Care to join us?"

"No thanks, Emmitt," Claire says. "We ate not too long ago. How about some coffee in the living room?"

"I'll get some," Maggie says and heads into the kitchen.

Claire and Lindsay follow Maggie, which leaves the two men standing in awkward silence in the foyer. Willis scrutinizes Emmitt with the trained eye of a retired family physician.

"How's your health?" asks Willis, breaking the silence. "Have you been to the doctor lately?"

"Uh, yeah," replies Emmitt. He clears his throat. "Why'd you ask?"

Willis steps closer and examines Emmitt with unblinking eyes. "Your skin is pale, and your face is thinner than the last time I saw you."

Emmitt's eyes dart around for help as Maggie and Claire pass between them. They carry mugs and saucers in hand while Willis holds Emmitt in his gaze.

Emmitt gestures to the living room. "Shall we, then?"

Willis grunts and leaves Emmitt standing in the foyer.

"Whoa!" Willis exclaims with sudden glee. "Look at all these lights and decorations." He glances at his granddaughter and smiles. "Lindsay Jane, I bet you did all this."

"Yup," replies Lindsay. "Mommy and Daddy helped, too."

When Willis and Claire sit on the couch, Lindsay joins them. She snuggles between her grandparents to get just enough room.

"Lindsay, aren't you hungry?" Maggie asks.

"Nope," Lindsay says. "I wanna stay here with Gramma and Grampa."

Emmitt and Maggie exchange smiles and return to the kitchen by themselves. At the table, the clinking of forks and knives upon glassware passes between Emmitt and Maggie. Both have turned their ears to the sing-song voice of Claire. She tells a story to Lindsay to pass the time while Emmitt and Maggie finish breakfast.

Maggie stops eating. She puts down her utensils. Leaning forward, her arms resting on the table, she gazes at Emmitt.

"What?" Emmitt asks with a mouthful of food.

"I love you," Maggie replies sweetly.

Emmitt swallows. "I love you, too." When Maggie's gaze doesn't waiver, Emmitt stops eating. "What now?"

"You tell me," she says.

Emmitt steals a glance in the living room. Willis, sitting on the sofa, takes a sip of coffee and casts a watchful eye at Emmitt

"Your father?" Emmitt asks. Maggie smiles and nods. In return, Emmitt relays the observation Willis made about his appearance. Her smile fades.

"I guess I hadn't noticed," says Maggie. "Except for last night, you've had no issues, have you?"

"Well," says Emmitt. He shifts in his seat, feeling his heartbeat rapidly in his chest as his jaw tightens. He breathes slowly and steadily as he stares at his food, avoiding his wife's eye contact. While Maggie waits, she gives the table a rhythmic rap of her fingers.

Jingling and tiny feet pattering across the floor, interrupts this battle of wills.

Lindsay squeals. "Mommy and Daddy! Let's open presents!"

Emmitt flashes Maggie a weak smile. "Talk later?"

Maggie exhales and turns to her daughter. "Daddy'll be along shortly. He's not feeling well, so he'll take his time, won't he?" She gives Emmitt a knowing look.

"Yeah," Lindsay says.

Maggie takes Lindsay's outstretched hand, leaving Emmitt alone in the kitchen.

Emmitt studies the scene in the living room — his daughter beaming with joy as Maggie reaches the Christmas tree, kneels, and hands a present to Lindsay. "Hey, Emmitt!" Willis calls. "Are you gonna join us or study us?"

Pushing his plate away, Emmitt stands. A mild prick of pain creeps into his right leg. He shakes this off in a few short strides through the foyer. His stomach knots in anticipation of the scrutiny from Willis and now Maggie during what should be a joyous exchange of gifts.

Once seated, Emmitt catches Willis watching him for a moment before the man's gaze returns to the center of the attention. Lindsay Jane is opening a present from her grandparents. Emmitt smiles, and across from him, he catches his wife's gaze. Her eyes are bright. She brushes a loose strand of hair from her face and tucks it behind an ear, only to have it flop back over her face again as she bends over to help Lindsay with a tightly knotted bow. From his back pocket, Willis pulls out a knife and slices the bow, freeing Lindsay to shred the shiny gift wrap to reveal a doll, which Emmitt vaguely recalls someone, maybe Maggie, mentioning the toy on Lindsay's wish list.

Another round of gifts commences, and each gift is opened one at a time so that all eyes could be attentive to the ceremonial giving and receiving of each gift. Lindsay, caught in the magic of the day, finds every moment a cause for rapturous joy, which she shows each time with a squeal upon opening the present. Then jumping up, she runs and wraps her arms around the giver in complete gratitude. This, more than anything, brings Emmitt joy despite his brow clammy with cold perspiration and his right leg, twinging in torment.

With the morning's festivities ending, Emmitt takes a break to stand. He stretches and limps toward the window to catch a glimpse for the first time of the great cold outdoors. The snow is glazed over with a sheet of ice, smooth and unbroken, covering even where he and Lindsay had romped through the snowy yard the day before.

"It's certainly quite a sight," Willis says from behind him.

Emmitt winces at the presence of his father-in-law but manages to nod as he continues to look out the window.

"I've been watching you, Emmitt," Willis says quietly.

Emmitt turns toward Willis and looks him in the eyes. "Thanks, pop," he says flatly.

Willis doesn't back down. "You're dizzy and pale. Are you on something?"

"No." Emmitt steps away from Willis. "But thanks for your concern. I'm gonna lay down." He leaves his father-in-law in the foyer and heads to the kitchen where Maggie cleans up. "I'm going upstairs. I'm not feeling well."

Without waiting for her reply, he makes his ascent and enters the cool undecorated darkness of the master bedroom. Sitting down at the end of the bed, Emmitt contemplates the contents of the bottle hidden in the bathroom wall.

Floorboards creaking in the hallway announce a visitor. Emmitt stands to brace himself for a lecture from his father-in-law. Intent on meeting him in the hallway, Emmitt steps toward the door only to be overtaken by a sudden spell of dizziness. He crashes to the floor.

As darkness overtakes him, Emmitt mumbles, "Merry Christmas to me."

Heavy footsteps approach. Willis kneels beside Emmitt. With the cool and practiced touch of a physician's hand, he checks for a pulse and the breath of life.

Willis calls out. "Maggie! Call an ambulance." Under his breath, Willis hisses. "Stay with us, you selfish bastard."

Chapter Five

June 20, 2000

Six months later, Emmitt sits in his dorm room with a duffle bag packed and ready to go. With dread and longing, Emmitt imagines his homecoming—the congratulations from friends and family and the awkward silence between him and Maggie when the party ends, and the guests have all gone home. Despite countless hours of therapy, he wrestles with one word: failure.

His heartbeat quickens, and tears threaten to fall for the third time today. A knock at the door pulls Emmitt from his funk. He looks up to see Father Klein leaning against the door frame, one hand in his pocket.

"You ready, Emmitt?" the priest asks.

Emmitt studies the floor. "I don't know if I can go back, Father."

Father Klein takes a seat. "Look, Emmitt. I'm not going to pretend it's going to be easy. I could offer the cliché responses. But you know God's grace is enough, especially in our weaknesses."

Emmitt nods, recalling the weekly sessions between

him and Father Klein. He'd been a lifeline, helping him to connect with God, family, and himself.

Father Klein continues. "Let me ask you this. Who has called you every night? Who has visited you every day?"

Maggie's constant presence by his side and her love for him comes to mind. Still, Emmitt can't bring himself to say her name.

Father Klein stands. "If you don't know it already, you need to know it now. There is nothing you could do that will cause your wife Maggie to love you any less. If anything, I think she may love you even more in your brokenness, not because of your brokenness, but because you've nothing to hide behind. You've nothing to lean upon, but God's grace and the woman he has put in your life."

Emmitt combs his fingers through his hair. "You're right. Maggie is... amazing. It's just..." His voice trails off as he struggles to put words to what he already knows. Maggie has sacrificed a lot, maybe too much, for him.

"You'll see," Father Klein says. "Know that I will be praying for you, and we can continue meeting even though you are leaving this place." As Father Klein turns to leave, Emmitt stands.

"Wait," he blurts. Father Klein pauses, and Emmitt takes a deep breath. "Thank you, Father, for everything." He extends his hand to Father Klein, and the two men embrace.

Father Klein leaves the room as Emmitt sits back down. He looks around his room for what he hopes to be the last time. The space resembles a monastic cell with its poorly cushioned chair, a small wooden desk, and a twin-size bed with springs that squeak the moment a man lays upon it until the moment he gets up in the morning. Oddly, Emmitt realizes, he will likely miss the simplicity of the old spring mattress more than anything else about this place. He sighs, reaches into his bag, and pulls out a prayer book and a rosary, both of which

Father Klein had given him at his first meeting with him. Emmitt opens the prayer book and reads Father Klein's inscription on the inside:

Draw near to the throne of grace, that you may receive mercy and find grace to help in time of need.

Beneath the humming of the white light, Emmitt prays quietly and moves his fingers along the beads. His right leg shakes involuntarily, and the clock ticks, seemingly on purpose, in opposite time with the shaking of his leg. Yet he prays. Rather than focus on the anxiety he feels about going home or the growing pain in his leg, Emmitt offers his troubles to God, who has given him grace. Emmitt has already come to learn that God is indeed sufficient for him.

Another knock at the door interrupts Emmitt's prayers. He opens his eyes to see Maggie standing at the door and gazing at him. She wears her long, brown hair in a loose bun. She wears a blue denim shirt with rolled sleeves, and her pale, blue eyes glisten beneath the harsh light of the humming bulb above them. She smiles slightly and steps toward him.

Emmitt stands. He shifts his weight, not certain of whether he should step toward her and hug her or wait until she makes the first move.

"I—" he begins.

Maggie places a delicate finger up to his lips. She takes his face in her hands, brushes up against him, and kisses him. Like a hasty schoolboy, Emmitt passionately returns kiss for kiss. Just as suddenly as it began, it ends with Maggie taking a step back and offering Emmitt her loving gaze.

"I've missed you," she whispers. Her face glows. She bites her lower lip, waiting for a reply.

"I'm sorry," Emmitt says hoarsely.

Maggie shushes him. "I've forgiven you, and it's time to come home."

Emmitt sighs. "I love you, Maggie."

Maggie chuckles. "I know. Your daughter's waiting

for you." The couple signs out of the building and head home.

* * *

Upon his arrival home, Emmitt smiles when he sees an array of colorful balloons knotted to the mailbox and dancing in the breeze. Above the front porch, a bright, red banner with white lettering that says, "Welcome Home!"

Aside from the flapping of the banner and the dancing of the balloons, Emmitt observes no sign of life appearing on the property or within the home. Maggie pulls into the driveway, shuts off the engine, and turns to him. Her blue eyes sparkle as she smiles and leans into him with a kiss. His otherwise steady heartbeat begins to beat more rapidly as he is rapturously caught up in this moment, causing the balloons and the banner to dissolve until his only thought is the love of his life, Maggie.

She pulls away and smiles. Her cheeks flush. "Shall we go in?" she asks.

Emmitt nods and reaches for the duffle bag on the floor behind him. As they walk up the front porch, Emmitt follows a few paces behind Maggie as though he is a potential suitor filled with the hope and the uncertainty of acceptance into the family.

Maggie jingles the keys as she unlocks the door, which she opens up on the silent darkness of an apparently uninhabited house. As Emmitt follows her through the threshold, the lights flicker on, and the silence is ruptured by joy as each member, making up their circle of family and friends, embrace him and welcome him back. Among these, of course, is Lindsay Jane. Emmitt hugs her and lifts her up to carry her through the small crowd until he sits on the couch, holding his daughter in his lap with his wife by his side.

This is a picture-perfect moment: Emmitt sitting with

his daughter in his lap and Maggie nestling beside him, with her arm around him. Yet, like any picture which captures a moment in time, the viewer could not possibly zoom into the heart of the subject. In this case, it is Emmitt who, though surrounded by loving support, holds his daughter like a shield over his heart, hoping to mask his misgivings and his fear, for when the party is over, it will just be himself, in need of support from his wife and daughter. And himself with the overwhelming feeling of being incapable of returning the support.

"Hey, Emmitt," Frank says.

Emmitt refocuses and looks up to see his friend looking down at him. As Emmitt stands to greet him, Lindsay hops up.

"Hey, princess, why don't you go say hi to Troy?" Emmitt asks.

In the next room, Leo Andreadis' son Troy stands by his father. He is dark, lean, and tall for his nine or ten years of age. He nudges his daughter in Troy's direction.

As Emmitt stands upright to shake Frank's hand, he watches as Lindsay runs to Troy. She chats with Troy in animated excitement for a moment before taking his hand and inviting him to sit. Lindsay pours Troy a glass of soda. Leo, Troy's father, returns Emmitt's watchfulness with a smile and a nod.

"They're great together," Emmitt says when he sees Troy and Lindsay sit at the kid's table.

"Kids," Frank says with a laugh. "Daniella and I never had them after her miscarriage, but we love your daughter as if she were our own."

Emmitt hugs his friend. "Thank you for taking care of her and Maggie these last few months."

"It's been great, given the circumstances." Frank smiles. "Just like before, I'm not going anywhere."

"I know that, Frank. I gotta be honest." Emmitt scratches his head. "I just don't want to mess it up again. I don't know how much more of this bullshit Maggie can take."

Frank simply nods and sits. A moment later, he is joined by Daniella, who hands him a drink and gives Emmitt a hug.

"We're just glad your home, and I know Maggie is, too," says Daniella.

As Emmitt sits, he glances at the kids. Though they are three years apart, Lindsay and Troy chat like they're best friends. As Maggie takes a seat between the kids, she smiles and waves at Emmitt.

Frank claps Emmitt on the shoulder. "I don't think you have anything to worry about, Emmitt. She's gonna be around for a very long time."

Sitting back on the sofa, Emmitt begins to relax because he trusts Frank's judgment. Frank and Daniella have been in his life for years and have experienced a great deal of tragedy themselves. Yet, even with this knowledge, Emmitt's conscience is pricked as he excuses himself from the couch.

"I have to take care of something upstairs," he says quickly.

Once in the master bedroom, Emmitt looks to the bathroom, determined to flush the demon once and for all from his life. For how could he come back to this home and live here, knowing that at any moment he could fall back to the bottle? However, once he opens the cabinet, he sees that everything's changed. There is a sealed removable paneling, and Emmitt assumes the bottle is disposed.

"Is everything, okay?" Maggie asks.

Emmitt turns to see her standing with her arms crossed in front of the doorway.

"Yeah, I guess," Emmitt says.

"Let's have a seat."

Maggie sits on the edge of the bed and pats the spot beside her. Emmitt joins her.

"After you were admitted to the hospital and stabilized, Frank, Daniella, and I found these," says Maggie. She produces the pill bottle with a shake. "Then we sealed up the cabinet. I was gonna talk about this when everyone had left, but—"

"I jumped the gun," Emmitt interjects as he finishes Maggie's sentence.

Maggie nods and continues. "Are there any other places in the house? I love you too much to see you go through this again. I also don't think I can go through this again."

Emmitt shakes his head. "There are no other places. I was gonna dump these and quit."

"Okay, here you go." Maggie places the bottle in Emmitt's hands.

Emmitt grips the bottle in his hand. "I'm sorry for not telling you, Maggie. I'm sorry for everything."

When she doesn't respond, he stands and walks toward the bathroom. He pops the bottle open. He dumps the remaining pills into the toilet. With a quick flush, the pills spiral down the drain and disappear forever from Emmitt's life.

He returns to Maggie's side on the bed, where she pulls him close and kisses his cheek.

"I forgive you," she says. "Now, let's return to the party. I think they're getting ready to cut the cake."

After a guest cuts the cake, Emmitt receives the first piece. The room erupts with a cheer. At the conclusion of the festivities, family and friends offer their support as they leave. Maggie and Emmitt gratitude with smiles and *thank-yous*.

* * *

That evening, Emmitt and Maggie sit with Lindsay as she lies in bed. "Daddy," Lindsay says, "I'm glad we're a family again."

"I'm glad we are, too," says Emmitt. He puts his arm around Maggie and brushes his hand across Lindsay's hair.

"Tell me a story," Lindsay says.

Beginning with a brave, wounded knight, Emmitt tells the story of how he battles one monster after the next, so he can rescue a beautiful princess. She is locked away in a lonely tower in the middle of a dark forest guarded by a dragon. As he tells the story, Maggie kisses him on the cheek and exits the room, leaving Emmitt alone with his daughter to finish the tale. When he finishes, he kisses his sleeping daughter upon her forehead and pulls the comforter closer to her.

"Good night, my little princess," he whispers.

CHAPTER SIX

September 5, 2003

"There's no need for the money," Emmitt yells as he stands from the kitchen table and nearly knocks his coffee mug to the floor.

"It's not the money," Maggie says quietly. "It's my sanity."

"Your sanity, really?" Emmitt scoffs. "Who's been here day and night, going to rehab and trying to keep this demon at bay? Don't you talk to me about sanity."

Maggie steps toward him. "Em. You need a purpose in your life. Yeah, you make it to all of Lindsay's soccer games, but what else do you do to fill the time besides cleaning your gun and hanging at the donut shop? You're not an old man."

Emmitt sits. His leg begins to shake as this statement nags at him. Phantom pains seem to gnaw at his leg. A moment ago, if not for his wife, he would have let loose.

"I'm sorry," Emmitt says quietly. "I just can't get a job right now."

"The manager at the arts and crafts store offered me a full-time job," Maggie says firmly. "I'm taking it."

Emmitt's eyes grow wide as he searches Maggie's face for an explanation. She crosses her arms and returns his gaze. There is not a hint of bluffing.

"I didn't know you were looking for a full-time job," Emmitt says.

"I guess you haven't been listening either," Maggie says shakily. She sounds as if she's about to cry, but she refrains. "I'm going to finalize the paperwork today." Maggie leans over Emmitt and kisses him. "I love you, Emmitt, but I need a change. I thought these past few years with you moving from rehab to therapy would get you out of this slump, but now I'm not sure. Like I told you before, the money from your settlement will run out. You need to do something soon."

"I know," Emmitt says. "I'll look for work tomorrow."

"That's what you always say." Maggie gasps. "I'm sorry. I didn't mean to say that."

Emmitt smiles weakly. "It's okay."

Emmitt sits before Maggie like a ghostly knight before his queen. He's cladded in rusty armor, guarding a crumbling castle, yet incognizant of the decay he wears and defends.

"I'll be back soon," Maggie says. "You want to come?"

Emmitt shakes his head. "I'll wait up for Lindsay's school bus to drop her off. I'll make dinner."

As Maggie leaves, Emmitt's shoulders seem to slump even more. He realizes he's stuck and can no longer continue to exist with the moments between moments. Still, he decides to put his thoughts on hold to prepare for the evening ahead.

CHAPTER SEVEN

October 15, 2003

Upon the top row of a set of bleachers three rows high, Emmitt sits enjoying the crisp autumn afternoon air. He wears his freshly pressed security guard uniform. Like the air around him, the uniform seems to invigorate him, making him sit a little taller. Though the security gig only pays minimum wage, it's a job that works with Maggie's schedule. He'd meet her at the soccer games. She'd drive Lindsay home while he took the van to his overnight job.

He stands when activity on the left side of the field catches his attention. Lindsay, with her soccer team, begins her warm-up exercises before an intramural scrimmage. Though other sets of parents have taken their seats in the rows in front of him, Emmitt is alone. He checks his watch. It's four-sixteen in the afternoon. Maggie should be off work and at the field by now. Emmitt twists in his seat and scans the parking lot. Seeing that other parents are still arriving, he removes his security guard jacket and lays it on the seat beside him. Then, he shifts his attention to the right side of the playing field. Without a pause in her jumping jacks, Lindsay waves and smiles at him. He waves back and stops when there is a tap on his shoulder.

Turning around, Emmitt meets the broad bearded smile of Leo Andreadis. During the process of ironically sponsoring Leo throughout the course of a twelve-step program four years ago, Emmitt got to understand Leo very well. Throughout his terrible divorce, Leo's frequent turn to booze eventually led to his alcoholism and subsequent loss of a custody battle over his only son Troy.

Emmitt could relate to Leo's addiction, but he kept to himself the notion that but for the grace of God and the support of Maggie and Frank, his own marriage would have easily gone down that road. Like repaying a debt he owed to the world, Emmitt chose to forgive Leo and become his sponsor. Over the last four years, they have formed an honest friendship.

"Is this seat taken?" Leo asks.

"Yeah, it is," Emmitt says. He removes his jacket from the seat. "But you can sit here until Maggie arrives."

Leo climbs up from the back of the bleachers and takes the seat next to Emmitt. For a moment, the two men sit next to each other in silence and watch the scrimmage begin. When Lindsay kicks the ball down the field, Emmitt stands and cheers her on toward the goal. When an opposing player kicks the ball from her, Emmitt sits again and notices that Leo is not really watching the game. Instead, his focus seems to be on a game happening on the adjacent field.

"So, you're not here to watch Lindsay play," Emmitt says.

"Nope, you got me," Leo says with a chuckle. "I'm here to watch my son play."

"So, he's in town?" Emmitt asks. "I thought he was just here a couple of weekends a month."

"There's a game today, but his mother is there as well." Leo huffs. "Don't want to get into that mess."

Emmitt nods. "How's Troy taking it?" When Leo doesn't answer, Emmitt clears his throat. "You know that you two are welcome over anytime. I'm sure Lindsay would enjoy seeing Troy."

At this, a smile tugs at the corner of Leo's mouth. "I think he would like that. I...we appreciate the offer."

"Anytime, Leo." Emmitt returns his attention to the game. The noise of the field and fans lulls away each uncomfortable minute passing between the two men. Emmitt checks his watch.

"Traffic must be heavy," he says. "I need to call Maggie's work. Can you watch Lindsay for a bit?"

Leo nods, and Emmitt lifts and pivots in his seat, exiting the bleachers from the rear. He makes his way to a one-story brick building housing the field restrooms, the announcer's booth, and a payphone. Once there, he drops in a quarter and dials Maggie's work.

"How can I direct your call?" asks a woman in a cheery tone on the other end.

"It's me," replies Emmitt. He mentally kicks himself for being so jittery. There's no way the receptionist would know who he was. "This is Emmitt Wasson. Can I speak to Maggie?"

There is a half second of silence on the other end of the phone before the woman responds. "I'm sorry, Mr. Wasson. She was rushed to the hospital fifteen minutes ago."

"What?" Emmitt tightly grips the receiver. "Why didn't you call?"

"We did, sir. No one answered at home, but I can tell you she's at Memorial."

"Thanks." After slamming the phone down, Emmitt rushes to the bleachers to his friend. "Hey, Leo. I've gotta run to the hospital to see Maggie."

"Shit," Leo says. "What happened? I mean. Let me know if you need anything."

"I will." Leo opens his mouth to say speak, but Emmitt nods and jogs away before he can hear what he has to say.

Making his way around the field, he approaches Lindsay's coach and tells her that he needs to take her away for a family emergency. Seconds later, a timeout is called, and she sends in a sub. Lindsay jogs to the sidelines.

"What's up, coach?" Lindsay asks between breaths as she grabs a green jug filled with water. She chugs the water.

"Your dad's taking you away early," her coach says. "Sorry, kiddo."

"But I want to—"

"It's mom," Emmitt cuts her off. "Grab your bag. We gotta go to the hospital."

Knowing that Lindsay would follow close behind him, Emmitt sprints to the van. He starts the engine just as Lindsay slides open the back door, tosses her bag on the floor, and pulls the seat belt over her chest and waist. Before even hearing the click, Emmitt speeds out of the parking lot.

"Dad, slow down!" Lindsay yells. "I'm not even buckled!"

"Sorry," Emmitt says.

He pushes the break, and the van slows to a halt. Behind him, he hears the click of Lindsay's belt, and he glances in the rearview mirror. When he catches his daughter's eyes, he turns around and gives her a weak smile.

"Mom'll be okay," he says reflexively. "We'll be okay." Emmitt seems to be speaking more to his own doubts than to his daughter, who frowns and looks back at her teammates playing on the field.

Turning his attention back to the road, Emmitt gently presses his foot on the gas. After checking his mirrors again, he pushes the gas pedal, and the van accelerates until it reaches its top speed. Within seconds, Emmitt stirs a whirlpool of tension and fear as he plays over in his mind Maggie's first emergency visit to the hospital just seven years ago. Though his daughter was too young to vividly remember that moment, she is very much aware of her mother's heart condition.

Driving on, he glances once again in the rearview mirror. Lindsay's bright blue eyes, so much like Maggie's, are filled with tiny pools. She blinks, and a tear rolls down her cheek, pulling with it some grime from the playing field.

Turning his attention back to the road, Emmitt wonders if perhaps he should have left Lindsay behind to finish playing. He could have left her with Leo. But then again, Leo seemed to have something else on his mind, a question or a favor that Emmitt had brushed off with a quick sprint. With a shake of his head, Emmitt pushes this thought to the back of his mind, deciding that if it is important, Leo would certainly ask him later.

With nothing else to focus on, but the driving and his wife, Emmitt grits his teeth, grinding out a series of thoughts: *Why is she in the hospital again? Why is God letting this happen? Why?* These thoughts spiral into a silent prayer.

God, I can't do this alone. Not now. Not ever. Take us all or take none of us. Just please don't take Maggie. My wife. My love. My—

"Daddy, are we almost there?" asks Lindsay.

A second is all he needs to dam up the flood of tears and attempt to force reason to his lips.

"Just a few more blocks," Emmitt whimpers. He gasps as he fights back tears.

"Are you okay?"

He clears his throat. "Yes, I'm just a little thirsty, that's all."

Lindsay taps him on the side of his arm. Grabbing the water jug, Emmitt pops open the top with his teeth and drinks.

"I hope the doctors can fix her," Lindsay says.

"Me, too, princess," says Emmitt. He hands back her bottle.

While at a stoplight, he glances at Lindsay and sees the care she takes to secure the bottle in the mesh pouch on the outside of her duffle bag. While other kids her age would be inclined to jam it in there, Lindsay slides the bottle back in place and smooths out the crinkles in the bag before zipping it up. A touch of nostalgia passes over Emmitt as he smiles. Lindsay is like Maggie in so many ways.

* * *

"Hey, we're here," Emmitt says, pulling into the hospital parking lot.

When he parks, he turns off the van and, being the first one out, meets Lindsay at the sliding passenger door. Before the door locks into place, Lindsay jumps out. Emmitt looks at her feet. A thin layer of mud is caked to her cleats and scattered around her feet in small chunks.

"You can't go in like that," protests Emmitt. "Why didn't you change in the car?"

"I don't know," says Lindsay as she shrugs. "We were in a hurry."

"Well, stomp your feet as you go and bring your duffle bag. You can change inside."

With his daughter following behind him and stomping out cakes of mud and grass over the parking lot, Emmitt makes his way to the front door of the hospital, where the sliding glass doors open. At the front desk of the hospital lobby, a female attendant is on the phone. Behind him, he hears his daughter's cleats click on the linoleum floor. She stands beside him, with her duffle bag over her shoulder.

Emmitt places his arm around Lindsay and pulls her close.

"Thank you for your patience, sir," the attendant says.

"No problem," Emmitt says. "My wife came in, maybe an hour ago. Her name is Margaret Wasson."

After a few keystrokes, the attendant addresses

Emmitt. "She's in the O.R. Third floor."

Emmitt nods and leads Lindsay towards the elevators. "Where're we going?" Lindsay asks. "Is Mommy going to be okay?"

The elevator door opens, and Emmitt leads his daughter in. As the elevator door closes shut, the reflection of an unrecognizable man gazes back at Emmitt. Lindsay Jane stands by his side, clutching his hand. He struggles to keep it together, but he sees that his armor is cracking, breaking under the weight of uncertainty. He closes his eyes, blinking back the heat of tears. One tear escapes and rolls down his cheek. He wipes it away with the cuff of his shirt. When he opens his eyes again, he sees his princess beside him. She wears a soccer uniform. There is a streak of mud extending from her uniform down to her sock, bulging with a shin guard. He wraps his arm around her, pulling her closer to himself.

"Daddy," she says. "I've got you."

"I've got you," Emmitt says.

The elevator door slides open, and the reflection vanishes. Lindsay exits, leading Emmitt toward another attendant, who smiles when they approach.

"I'm here about my wife," says Emmitt as his voice cracks. "Margaret Wasson."

"Hey, Emmitt and Lindsay," Daniella's voice calls.

Turning, Emmitt sees Frank and Daniella standing in the waiting room. Lindsay, dropping her bag, runs to them and embraces Daniella first and then Frank. Emmitt does the same.

"Have you heard anything?" Emmitt asks.

"Nothing," Frank says. "We've been waiting for about an hour already."

"Hey, Lindsay," Daniella says. "Why don't we get you cleaned up a little?"

Lindsay nods and grabs her duffle bag. She follows Daniella to the restroom.

"Emmitt, I need you to listen," Frank says. "Maggie

was in a very bad accident on the way to the soccer game. Another car plowed into the driver's side at a very high speed just as she was leaving work. It's bad. I need you to know that."

Hearing this information, guilt penetrates Emmitt's being. If he'd not waited until Maggie had no other choice than to go to work, there would be no way she ever would have been in such a situation. Emmitt breathes deeply as time for him passes into vast uncertainty. He sits, unwilling to give credence to his perceived truth through a voiced confession.

With Daniella by her side, Lindsay returns in clean shoes and socks. She lays her head on Emmitt's lap. Frank sits to Emmitt's right. In another time, Emmitt's attention would have been drawn to his leg, blasting out phantom pains that would beckon him to turn once again to a pill. Today he turns his attention away from himself to focus on his daughter's well-being.

Though he begins to feel his leg ache, more for the need to escape the dread than for actual pain, Emmitt focuses his attention elsewhere: prayer and the God who hears and understands human suffering. Lacking words of his own, save for the deepest desire for his wife to pull through, he bows his head.

"God," he whispers, "grant me the serenity to accept the things I cannot change, courage to change the things I can, and wisdom to know the difference."

With his prayer finished, Frank, Daniella, and Lindsay take hold of his hands. Together they sit in silent anticipation.

Sometime in the late evening hours, a weary and matted haired doctor enters the waiting room. He brushes back his hair as he scans the room.

"Mr. Wasson," the doctor says.

Standing, Emmitt shifts his sleeping daughter, who awakens with a groan.

"Is Mommy coming home?" Lindsay asks.

The doctor grimaces and takes a step back. Emmitt

approaches.

"I'm sorry, sir," the doctor says quietly. "She didn't make it. There was just too much damage."

At the doctor's words, obliterating guilt and sorrow bears upon Emmitt. He staggers back, seeking solace in a seat. Frank puts an arm around him, catching his weight and guiding him to a chair.

"We're right here for you," he replies.

"It's no use," pants Emmitt. His sobs turn back the titillating tide of guilt churning within his heart. None of his party, including his own daughter, could possibly know what lurks beneath the surface of his own sorrow. Lindsay buries her face into Emmitt's jacket and cries until her own misery moistens, then soaks through to his heart.

Though surrounded by such strong support, Emmitt knows with certainty that he is alone. The burden of guilt is his own. Saturated by his own tears and that of his daughter's, his prayers for serenity threaten to succumb to despair, and he wishes in this very moment that his marriage with Maggie had ended like Leo's. At least then, Maggie would still be alive

Chapter Eight

October 18, 2003

Buried beneath the layers of hardened armor lies a wellspring of emotion seeking the smallest crack, cinched tight by the tiniest of tenacity clutched within Emmitt's shattered heart. At church, with his daughter to his right, and Frank and Daniella to his left, he is determined to be an unyielding fortress gripped together despite his need to break and pour forth a fountain of tears. Lindsay Jane does exactly what he would like to do. Tears stream down her cheeks as she whimpers quietly. He pulls her close as Father Klein steps to the pulpit to deliver the homily.

"In today's reading, Jesus calls all who are weary to come to Him. For in your weariness, he will give you rest. Today, though a loved one, Margaret Wasson, has passed away, Jesus is still by your side, saying, 'Blessed are the poor in spirit, for theirs is the kingdom of God...'"

As Father Klein's pass over him, Emmitt shuts himself off from the idea of somehow being blessed because Maggie is gone. He looks to Lindsay. She has stopped crying and is listening intently to the priest. He returns his attention to the pulpit.

"...we will miss her severely and for many of you," Father Klein pauses to scan the congregation until he locks eyes with Emmitt. "For many of you, your burden will be much greater, but look to those around you. They are the hands and feet of Christ Himself, who tells us today that his yoke is easy, and his burden is light. This is because you are not alone. Not one bit. Let us pray."

As Father Klein prays, heartache and contrition override Emmitt's very being. Frank places an arm around his shoulder.

"Like I said before, we're here for you," he says. "All of us." Frank nods.

Shoulders shaking, Emmitt stands with the rest of the congregation as he begins to cry.

The remainder of the mass, along with the burial and reception are a miserable blur of vaguely familiar people. They give their condolences with a hug and a few words. For a flashing, vivid moment, Emmitt wonders if the person that caused the accident would show up. Perhaps then there could be a transference of blame.

"Dad," says Lindsay as she squeezes his hand. "We'll get through this together."

In response, he nods, and this moment of lucidity fades once again to an endless and tiring vague charade of receiving and being received by people who he knows will not be there for him and Lindsay when it really, truly counts.

CHAPTER NINE

October 23, 2003

Though it is a cool autumn morning, Emmitt sits at a window in a dark living room. He is tired of the miserable monotony each day has brought him. Almost every day someone from church stops by to "check in on him" and bring him another homemade casserole that sits in the refrigerator, cold and uneaten.

As the stairwell behind him creaks, he stands to greet Lindsay before she leaves for school. Her blonde hair is done up in two ponytails that flank either side of her face.

She smiles weakly at him.

"Are you going to be okay today?" Lindsay asks.

"I will," Emmitt says. He pulls his daughter close and pecks her on the forehead. "You take care of yourself, princess."

She nods. "Can I have lunch money?"

Emmitt digs in his pockets and hands her a few dollars.

"Thanks," Lindsay says. "Are you going back to work soon?"

"Soon," Emmitt says. "I'll see you after school. How about we have a green bean casserole tonight?"

Lindsay curls a lip. "Ewww, we had that last night."

"I'll think of something. I love you."

"I love you, too," Lindsay says. She opens the door and stands there for a moment. The cool air she lets in freshens the dankness of the house. "Okay, bye, Daddy."

When the door shuts, Emmitt sits once again at the window and watches as Lindsay boards the bus. If not for the bearer of the casserole and the casseroles themselves, Emmitt's only company throughout the day would be the solitude of self-condemnation eating away at him as though he were to be directly blamed for Maggie's death.

He stands, grabs a jacket, and gets in an old sedan soon after Lindsay is on the bus and off to school. The car seems to drive itself as it meanders slowly down one street and around the corner of another. A police officer would have interrupted Emmitt's aimlessness with a flick of sirens and flashing of lights, but no such intrusion occurs until a speed bump jars him into awareness. After pulling over, Emmitt gets out and walks the perimeter of the car until he sees that he has a flat.

"Shit!" He yells as he kicks the tire. He opens the trunk to retrieve the jack and the spare. Crouching beside the car, he begins to pump the jack.

"Need help with that?" someone behind him asks.

Emmitt turns to see Leo towering over him.

"Are you following me?" asks Emmitt.

Leo shrugs and looks around. "You're in my neighborhood. I was having a smoke on the front porch and saw you get out."

Emmitt stands and regards the neighborhood. "Huh. Well, let's get this tire fixed since you offered."

Huddling next to each other, Leo holds the flat tire steady as Emmitt loosens the bolts.

"How are you holding up?" Leo asks.

In response, Emmitt continues to work on one bolt at a time until they are all removed. When Leo replaces the flat with the spare, Emmitt avoids eye contact, hoping that this would be enough to sway away the undesired conversation. With the bolts tightened and the jack dropped, the two men stand and wipe grease from their hands onto their jeans.

"Thanks." Emmitt offers Leo a hand.

"Anytime," Leo says, taking Emmitt's hand.

Emmitt returns his tools and slams the trunk shut. Before he can reach the driver's seat, Leo sidesteps Emmitt.

"Say, Emmitt. I needed to ask a favor of you."

Though he is not in the mood for doing favors, Emmitt nods for him to go on. Leo clears his throat, scratches his beard, then runs his hand through his hair before he continues. When he speaks, it is like listening to the revving of an old engine refusing to turn over. At each halting interval, Emmitt raises his head and lowers it with tightened lips, suppressing his need to interrupt.

"I wanted to ask you..." Leo pauses. "There's a custody hearing, and I wanted to know if...if you could testify for me."

After hearing all this, Emmitt finds himself once again in awe. Leo never ceases to produce a need for a favor during the most unfortunate times for Emmitt. But he concedes anyway. "Sure, just give me the dates," Emmitt says flatly.

"Thank you, my friend," Leo says, stepping toward Emmitt with open arms. "I owe you one." Leo pulls him close, slapping him on the back. When Emmitt is released from Leo's clutches, he steps away and gets back in the sedan.

"Hey, I'll see you around." Before Leo can respond, Emmitt keys the ignition, leaving his acquaintance in the exhaust.

Driving into uncertainty and toward a much larger neighboring city, Emmitt leaves his sparsely populated rural town behind. As he drives, he passes construction zones occupying fields once plowed and prepared in years past for the next planting season. The former landowners of these once hopeful fields will no longer sow or plow. They will no longer provide fresh crops at the farmer's market for the residents of the neighboring communities. Those in the surrounding communities will have to now rely on the large box store scheduled to be "coming in the spring," according to the sign Emmitt whizzes by. Emmitt is driven by the absence of even a whim. Unlike the farmers, conceding to the offer of great financial gains, Emmitt drives like a shot in the dark. He heads into the city, forgetting his daughter and forgetting that he, the poor in spirit, is truly blessed by God.

* * *

Sitting in an anonymous corner of an anonymous bar, Emmitt voicelessly consults with a glass of warm beer and a double shot of whiskey. Yet, the longer he lingers, the less likely he seems able to reconcile the responsibility he has placed upon himself with the simple reality that another party is already bound solely and completely to the crime which caused Maggie's death. Guilt teases his conscience to place the entire cause of her death on a choice he made just a few years ago to simply exist one day to the next, holding down a part-time gig, simply because he could.

The other patrons of the bar mill about, drinking and conversing with each other. Occasionally, patrons catch Emmitt's attention with a nod, and they raise their glasses toward each other. The patron takes a spirited sip while Emmitt rests his untouched glass upon its faded, stained cardboard coaster.

The bar door chimes as it opens, and heavy boots approach Emmitt's table. Someone slides the chair away from the table and sits, but Emmitt doesn't bother looking up.

"What the fuck are you thinking?" Frank asks suddenly. Emmitt gives him a disinterested nod and returns his gaze to the two glasses sitting on the table before him.

Folding his arms and staring at Emmitt, Frank continues. "You know, those demons of yours aren't going to help you. How many have you had?"

"None," Emmitt says.

"Funny," Frank says. "The bartender said you bought several rounds."

Emmitt lets out a snort. "Good job, Sheriff. They were for the others."

Frank looks around, then touches the beer glass. "It's warm. It's also almost eleven o'clock. How long have you been here?"

Emmitt shrugs. "Maybe since the afternoon. I'm not really sure. I wasn't paying attention to the time. How'd you find me anyway?"

"Leo called my department just after you took off. He was worried. You didn't show to pick up Lindsay for soccer practice. That's when we got worried. I checked the only traffic camera in town."

"Damn, nabbed by technology."

"And I know you. I figured you might be at one of the bars."

"Now what?" Emmitt holds out his hands. "You gonna cuff me or take me back in? I think you're out of your jurisdiction."

Frank chuckles. "No, nothing like that. What the hell are you thinking? Daniella and I might be Lindsay's godparents, but we aren't her mother and father."

"Well," Emmitt says, barely above a whisper. "Her mother's gone. Or did you forget?"

"Fuck you, Emmitt!" Frank rises from his seat. "Think about someone other than yourself. Do you really think Maggie would want to see you like this, running away?"

"Damn," Emmitt says. "Maybe I should have a drink.

54

The beer's warm. Maybe I'll try the whiskey." With slow deliberation, Emmitt reaches for the glass, knowing this would just piss Frank off.

Frank snatches the glass. In one gulp, he downs the whiskey then slams the empty glass, top side down, onto the table. Emmitt laughs because he has easily baited Frank, a seasoned interrogator.

"Fine!" Frank gets up from the table. "You can deflect all you want. Maybe you need a hobby, or a full-time job. Maybe you want to end up like your buddy Leo, fighting a custody battle. I don't know. Until you get your shit together and deal with this, you're not gonna be any good to anyone, especially your daughter."

Dropping a few bucks at the bar, Frank heads toward the front door.

"Hey," says Emmitt as he stands, "I'm sorry."

Frank ceases his stride and regards Emmitt for a moment. "Save it. Yeah, I'm disappointed, but I'm not the one you need to apologize to." He opens the front door, and a shaft of glimmering streetlight battles the shadows within the bar.

"Where're you going?" Emmitt asks.

Frank scoffs but doesn't turn. "I'm going home where you should be right now."

The bar door slams shut; the shadows resume their normal course within the bar. They beckon him to his lone corner table where the amber of the glass of warm beer invites him to sit. Emmitt does so, knowing that to answer the call by raising and downing a glass, could mean certain death to him.

He sneers.

To go back down that path will mean that he will become a cause for any, and even all, members of his sparsely populated community to respond with gossip. He imagines people will talk about how devastated he is because of Maggie's death. Yet this he can live with, especially if he never returns. He cannot live with the accusatory way in which his in-laws, especially Willis, will likely take on the care of Lindsay. They will certainly see him as a selfish derelict. Alone, or even taken as a whole, these *what-ifs* are not enough to move Emmitt to action, to walk out the door, get in his car and drive home to Lindsay: his daughter, his princess, his only light in this world. Lindsay Jane, and the fear of not just disappointing her, but devastating her, are what moves Emmitt to choose. In taking a step toward the bar door, he chooses life.

Each day he will be reminded of his wife. Her presence will linger in the smell of the bedsheets and the divot where she once slept on the mattress. The entire house will, in every detail, give testimony: *Here lived Margaret Wasson.* And, already so much like her mother in appearance and manners, Lindsay Jane will be a constant reminder of Emmitt's first love.

Stepping out of the bar door and into the glow of the city's night, Emmitt understands the choice to die each day. He understands he must take up the burden of consorting with self-sacrifice each day. In doing so, he will keep Lindsay far from any knowledge that any action on his part could be traced on a continuum leading to Maggie being at the wrong place at the wrong time. She could never know, or even understand, this truth. He alone will bear it.

Beside the door, Emmitt shivers in the cold, autumn air as he listens to the life of the city in the way young couples walk by in whispers, in the way traffic blares a block away, and in the way, a sudden and loud burst of a horn feet away from him has the capacity to send his heart racing with a jolt.

"Hey, buddy, if you're leaving, I'd like that parking spot!" a driver yells from his open window.

Emmitt waves at the driver and gets in his sedan, then pulls away. Without hesitation, he heads south toward home, to memories of his wife, and to Lindsay.

CHAPTER TEN

October 24, 2003

As the morning light banishes the shadowy memories of the night, Emmitt awakens, rising from the couch, still dressed in yesterday's clothes. For some, a night's sleep often brings the mind clarity of thought. For Emmitt, a night's sleep simply passes just out of reach. Emmitt stands and tries to force himself awake with a stretch.

"Good morning, sunshine!" Willis' voice booms from the kitchen.

Emmitt cringes at the realization that his father-in-law is here, but he continues to stretch. "When did you get in?" he asks.

"Last night," Willis says, stepping into the living room with two mugs. "Sit and drink this. Here." Willis hands Emmitt some coffee. "We'll talk when you're ready."

Avoiding any eye contact that would suggest any readiness on his part to engage in conversation, Emmitt sits and sips the coffee while he gazes out the window. Outside, autumn leaves have covered the browning grass with shades of red, orange, and yellow. Just a few weeks ago, Maggie had commented on how pretty the leaves were when they blew in the wind and decorated the lawn. In response, he had told her how he and Lindsay would gather the best of these leaves and use them to decorate the fading carpet in the living room. She had laughed at the joke.

"Dammit," Emmitt says as tears well up in his eyes. "I miss her. Her smile. Her laugh. Her smell."

"I do too, son," Willis says. "We all do."

Emmitt waits for a follow-up lecture. He found the lecture in his father-in-law's silence. It also waits in the scene unfolding before their eyes through the front window overlooking the yard. Lindsay Jane's side ponytails bounce as she kicks up leaves and chases a frisbee sailing through the yard from an unseen location beyond their view. The frisbee lands, skips, then rolls through the leaves. Picking it up, Lindsay shakes out the leaves before lobbing it short. The frisbee misses its target and Troy Andreadis, Leo's son, runs to catch it. Troy takes the frisbee and tosses it a short distance.

Emmitt stands and walks to the window. A moment later, Willis joins him in watching Lindsay and Troy in play. Lindsay catches Emmitt's gaze and cheerfully waves at him. Emmitt returns her gesture with a weak lift of his hand. Lindsay lobs the frisbee again, and Troy catches it with ease and walks over to her. With a flick of the wrist, Troy demonstrates how to smoothly pass the frisbee.

"You should be out there," Willis says.

Emmitt shrugs, fully aware of the intended meaning: *he needs to be there for Lindsay.*

"How long are you staying in town?" Emmitt asks.

"That's up to you. Claire and I have no plans, not since she retired last year."

"Stay as long as you like, then," Emmitt says. "The company will certainly be welcome."

"We will. Have you thought about getting a full-time job?"

This suggestion sends Emmitt's thoughts to the

previous night, causing him to draw the conclusion that his father-in-law and Frank have been talking for quite some time. He suspects the conversations may have started a few days after the funeral, or even a few years after his own debilitating accident at work.

"I'll talk to my shift manager when bereavement is over," Emmitt says as he brushes past Willis.

Willis clasps his arm. "You're not going to like it, but you and Lindsay should try family grief counseling."

Emmitt stops just as he opens the door, but he doesn't face his father-in-law. "You're right. I don't like it, but I guess you gotta suffer if you really want to live." Emmitt snorts. "Isn't that what Father Klein suggested?" He slams the door, leaving his father-in-law inside and incapable of continuing the conversation.

Outside, the first person to greet Emmitt is Troy, who clutches the frisbee in his hand.

"Hey, Mr. Wasson," Troy says. "I was just teaching Lindsay to play."

Emmitt regards him for a second. Loss and hope rage a war in the boy's eyes. Loss over the divorce he's had to endure and hope for some form of reunification.

"Thanks, Troy," Emmitt says as he sits. "You come by anytime."

Troy nods and steps away as Lindsay, with some hesitation, comes over to Emmitt.

"Daddy," Lindsay says. "I thought I'd lost you, too."

Hearing this, Emmitt experiences a sudden heaviness of heart and soul. When he had run, he had done so selfishly, not even thinking about how this would impact his daughter. Now, seeing her in front of him, her deep, blue eyes examining his face and eyes, he realizes how much she sees through him. She is so much like her mother in that way. Emmitt sighs heavily and looks into her eyes.

"I'm sorry, princess," he says. "It'll never happen again."

"I think we need help, Daddy," Lindsay answers.

Emmitt sighs. "Yes. I think so, too."

So, the princess's words break through what little armor is left of the wounded knight. With nothing left to hold onto, Emmitt breaks down and cries. His daughter, his princess, squeezes him tight, while Troy looks on.

CHAPTER ELEVEN

September 8, 2005

Emmitt sits in a pale blue cushioned chair, one that seems far too hard for a half-hour session with his therapist, Dr. Lauren Philips. He sits across from her, offering her a blank stare.

"Can you repeat the question?" Emmitt asks.

Dr. Phillips scribbles something in her notebook, looks up at him, and smiles tightly. "Your wife died two years ago—"

"Two years, one month, and five days ago," Emmitt interjects.

"Yes, of course," Dr. Phillips responds. "How often do you think about Maggie and what her loss means to you?"

Emmitt frowns. "All the time. I don't think a moment goes by that I don't think about her." As tears well up in his eyes, he reaches for a tissue.

Dr. Phillips nods. "How do you think this has affected your daughter Lindsay?"

In the slipping silence, Emmitt struggles with this question. He thinks over the past two years. Two years of passively acknowledging that there is a problem and hoping that it will come to an end, despite not doing anything about it.

"We... I haven't talked to Lindsay much about her mom." Emmitt says at last.

Dr. Phillips nods, but doesn't say anything else. Emmitt recalls a recent comment Father Klein made to him in the confessional. One about having a choice to die to self that he might rise to new life rather than remain suspended in a state of self-absorption.

"I've been thinking so much about what her death means to me that I haven't asked Lindsay about it," says Emmitt. He sighs. "I thought maybe she didn't want to talk about it. That maybe it'll be better to leave Maggie's death in the past."

"So, you want Lindsay to move on, like you have?" Dr. Phillips asks.

Emmitt scoffs. "Obviously, I haven't... which means... yeah... I see what you're saying." Dr. Phillips gives another nod, and the therapy session ends until next time.

* * *

Emmitt and Lindsay sit together in Dr. Phillips' office. Silence passes like a gentle breeze between the three. Emmitt feels a slight chill. Still, he can see that neither Dr. Phillips nor Lindsay is in the least bit cold as they look at him in expectation. After a moment, Emmitt looks Lindsay in the eye.

"I thought I was protecting you by trying to keep Mom's death in the past."

"But it's not in the past," Lindsay says. "Not for any of us."

Of course, he recognizes the influence of therapy on his daughter. Though the words are hers, the ideas have their origin in Dr. Phillips.

"And her death will continue to be in the present until

you can share with each other exactly how you are feeling," chimes in Dr. Phillips. "We can do that here, or you can find time on your own. But to continue forward, you both must be able to do more than superficially talk to each other."

This idea leaves Emmitt stunned, for he knows that deep conversation with his daughter will require open honesty. Looking at his daughter, now at the tail end of twelve-years-old, he sees before him an ocean of longing as she reaches out to him with the gentle tide of love. He embraces her.

"What do you think, princess?" he asks. "Are you ready for this?"

Lindsay nods, saying, "Please, Daddy. But not right now. Later maybe?"

"Certainly," he says and kisses her on the forehead. As he does so, he realizes that if any conversation is to take place, he must be the one to initiate it. In the past, he had waited for his daughter to say something, but not anymore.

"I think that's all for now," Dr. Phillips says. "I'll see you both in your private sessions and then together in a few weeks."

After saying their thanks and goodbyes to Dr. Phillips, Emmitt and Lindsay leave. As they walk out the door, Emmitt smiles. He feels somewhat lighter, yet he still carries with him the burden of loss and guilt.

It is as though, he admits to himself, that he has somehow skirted around the topic entirely. As he walks out of the building and toward the van with Lindsay, he wonders if she is aware of this guilt as well. She returns his glance and smiles. Yet her eyes, a brighter blue in the light of the sun, conveys just a shadow of doubt. This doubt, he must lay to rest.

So, the call to confession tugs at his heart. To let go of the guilt, he realizes his need to submit to mercy. A well-timed shot like this, one in which he and Lindsay are both emotionally and mentally aligned, cannot be wasted. It must be now if he will be the affectionate and supportive father that Lindsay so desperately needs.

CHAPTER TWELVE

September 13, 2005

On a late summer afternoon, a warm breeze passes over the freshly mowed and painted soccer field. Removing his jacket, Emmitt takes a deep breath, and prepares for Lindsay's first game in the fall soccer season to start. Though only in seventh grade, her skills and maturity have qualified her to try out for the high school junior varsity team. Beating out even some of the sophomores, she has earned the right as a starting player. Emmitt couldn't be prouder of his princess. Even now, he stands in the bleachers to loudly cheer as Lindsay takes the field.

Lindsay shifts the ball around the opposing players as though she is a one-woman team, outwitting and besting each rival who comes between her and the goal. An opposing player goes in for a slide-tackle, but Lindsay maneuvers around her and passes the ball to another player on the team. Her teammate shoots and scores. Emmitt recognizes this player as Ashley, a high school freshman, who has taken Lindsay under her wing.

At halftime, Emmitt rises from his spot on the

bleachers to deliver his daughter a few tangerines. These he started to carry in his pocket to all her games last year when she told him how hungry she always is after playing. Last year his daughter hit a growth spurt, causing her to grow nearly afoot. Now, at five foot five, she is the same height as most of the other players on the team, and her pediatrician says she is still growing. It is no wonder she has such an edacious appetite, especially after a game.

Walking the sidelines toward his daughter's team, Emmitt feels a tap on his shoulder. He turns to see Troy Andreadis walking right next to him.

"Hey, Mr. Wasson!" Troy shouts, his face beaming with enthusiasm.

"How are you doing, Troy?" Emmitt asks as he places an arm around the boy's shoulder.

Over the past few years, Troy has become somewhat of a big brother to Lindsay, looking out for her after school. He even helps her with her homework, although Emmitt suspects Lindsay helps him, especially with the algebra.

"How's soccer going for you this year?" Emmitt asks.

"It's not," replies Troy. He shrugs. "I'm the placekicker for the football team."

"I didn't realize that. Your father must be proud."

Troy's expression grows dark. "Not really. We're not close. I've been spending more time with my mom because he's drunk most of the time." Troy's face softens. "Maybe you could come around and talk to him. That helped last time."

Guilt pricks Emmitt's heart. Troy is another victim of Emmitt's self-absorption these past few years.

"I'm sorry, Troy," says Emmitt. "I've been taking my wife's death pretty hard."

"I get it," Troy says flatly.

The boy does get it, Emmitt realizes. He's no stranger to pain, what with his parents getting a divorce when he was such a young age. In some ways, his loss is even worse with parents that never talk to each other, especially with a drunk, deadbeat bad.

"I'll check in on your father," Emmitt says. "I'll see what I can do to help."

"We'll see," Troy says and continues to walk with Emmitt.

"You coming over to support the team?" Emmitt asks.

Troy smirks. "Something like that. And to say *hi* to Lindsay."

Emmitt chuckles. "Why am I not surprised? I'm sure she'd love to see you."

As the pair approaches the team, Emmitt unintentionally blocks Troy from Lindsay's view.

"Hey, Dad!" cheers Lindsay.

She jumps up when she sees Emmitt bring out the game day tangerines. He holds them in open palms. As always, he closes his hands quicker than she can snatch a tangerine from them. Payment is in the form of a hug, and some of the other girls watch with fascination. Releasing Lindsay from her debt, Emmitt places a tangerine in each of her open palms. Her cheeks, which are still flushed from running the field, become dimpled as she smiles.

"Thanks, Dad," says Lindsay.

"You're welcome, kiddo. Great playing out there."

Lindsay nods excitedly at her father's praise until her attention is drawn just beyond him. Emmitt turns to see Troy. Though there are less than ten feet between Troy and Lindsay, Troy is grinning and waving at her.

"Hey, Lindsay," he says.

"Oh, hi, Troy," Lindsay says, and her cheeks flush to a brighter shade of red.

"I like the way you got around that slide tackle," Troy says. "Nice moves."

The whole team focuses on the exchange between Emmitt and Lindsay as the scene unfolds. This deliberate shift, accompanied by a few giggles, is not lost on Emmitt, who stands awkwardly between Lindsay and Troy.

Shifting his scrutinizing glance between the two grinning adolescents, Emmitt breaks their trance.

"Hey, I think halftime is just about up, princess," says Emmitt. "I'm sure the coach will want to get the team huddled up. See you after the game, Lindsay."

After patting his daughter on the shoulder, he makes his way back up the sidelines. He looks over his shoulder and realizes Troy still lingers near the girls.

"See ya, Lindsay!" he yells as the girls return to the field.

Emmitt marches up the sideline. He can hear the girls swooning over Troy. Moments later, Troy jogs up next to Emmitt as he makes his way to the bleachers.

Emmitt blocks his path. "What's with you and my daughter?"

"Oh, we're just friends, Mr. Wasson," Troy replies. "You've known that forever."

"I don't think her team would describe that as 'friends.' Not with all of that *oohing*."

Troy waves this off. "Nah. That's just girl stuff. It's nothing."

"Well, let's keep it as nothing," Emmitt says, putting an edge in his voice. "She's too young to date. What grade are you in?"

"Tenth grade," Troy says. He looks down and kicks at the grass, sending a dandelion bud sailing through the air. "We're not dating or anything. We're just friends." Troy looks up and makes eye contact with Emmitt.

Emmitt weighs his next words carefully. "You're three years apart. In seven years, that won't matter. Until then, I think you and my daughter should put the friendship on hold for a while."

Troy nods. "Yes, sir. I'm gonna leave now. See ya around… I guess." He stuffs his hands in his pockets.

"Wait, Troy," replies Emmitt. "I'm sorry, bud. I didn't mean you can't come by. We'll just reign the relationship back a little, okay?"

"Whatever, man," Troy says. "Sure, I'll stop by."

Troy heads down the sidelines. With a sigh, Emmitt makes his way back to his seat. The second half of the game begins, though Emmitt finds that his focus is not on the game, but on a dreadful conversation he is bound to have with his daughter.

* * *

At the end of the game, Emmitt waits by the van until he sees that Lindsay has high-fived every member of the team. Lindsay, still wearing her cleats, bounces up to him and gives him a big hug. Without the rest of her team and four times as many adults watching, this is far less awkward. Emmitt is glad to be alone with his daughter.

"Hey, princess," he says. "You really broke a few ankles out there today."

"Yeah, Dad," she says awkwardly. Her smile fades. "Hey, you don't have to bother with the tangerines."

"What's wrong? You were okay with them last year."

"I know, but the high school girls think the tangerines are weird. Ashley thinks it's cool that you visit me like that, though."

Taking all this in, Emmitt feels just the slightest twinge in his heart. His daughter is growing up, and there's nothing he can do about it. He decides to accept this change.

"Hey, no problem," says Emmitt. "As long as I can still pick you up from the game."

"Yeah, Dad, about that..." Lindsay looks back at the bus, where the team is beginning to file in. "After a big win like this, they usually go out for pizza. It's just different being on a high school team."

"It sounds like we both have some adjusting to do. Do you still want me to come to the games?"

Lindsay's blue eyes widen, and she responds with just a hint of a whine in her voice. "Of course, I want you at the games, Daddy."

There's my little girl, Emmitt thinks to himself. Though grown up in appearance and often showing signs of incredible maturity, Emmitt sees that she is still there, hiding behind the façade of a young woman.

Several yards behind Lindsay, the team bus has started up. Ashley waves. "Lindsay, you coming?"

Lindsay glances over her shoulder, then back at Emmitt. She bites her lower lip as she waits for his response. Emmitt cocks his head toward the bus.

"You better hurry," he teases. "I'll meet you back at the school."

"Oh, thank you, Daddy."

Lindsay gives him another hug, which Emmitt barely has time to return before she scampers to the bus. As her ride slowly rolls out the parking lot, Emmitt drops his shoulders, suddenly realizing the tension that had built up from his talk with Lindsay. With a stretch and a sigh, he relaxes his shoulders, but this does very little to relieve the tension.

* * *

The sky speaks of the coming night, yet enough daylight remains, so the puff of cumulus clouds sails on the pale blue sky above a scattering of cars, vans, and SUVs, sitting in the parking lot of the high school's sports complex. Inside one of the vans, Emmitt awakens with a jolt as the team bus comes to a halt with a squeal and a whoosh of its brakes. Brushing off a stray fry from his chest, Emmitt sits up and tosses a greasy McDonald's bag on the floor behind him.

When Lindsay was younger, the family would go to McDonald's together after her games. After Maggie died, Emmitt and Lindsay carried on the tradition. She would get a Happy Meal, and he would get a Big Mac. Afterward, they would both have an ice cream. There was nothing special about the meal, no big victory to celebrate. The two simply shared father-daughter time during dinner. He was going to miss those times.

The stream of teenage girls rushing out of the bus slows to a trickle. Each girl says her congratulatory goodbye to the others before parting ways. Some go to their own vehicles, but most go to their drowsy parents waiting to pick them up. The back door of the van opens, and Lindsay tosses her duffle bag onto the floor. Then, she slides the door shut and sits in the passenger seat by Emmitt.

"How was it?" Emmitt asks.

"It was good." She spots a fry on Emmitt's shirt and picks it up with a shake. "But I think you enjoyed your food more." She rolls down the window and tosses the French fry out.

"Very funny." Emmitt starts the car and maneuvers through some parked vehicles still awaiting the arrival of their lollygagging passengers. Lindsay turns on the radio and waves at some of her teammates as the van exits the parking lot onto the main road. After a few blocks, Emmitt clears his throat.

"So, tell me about Troy," he says.

Lindsay rolls her eyes and groans. "Really, Dad? You've known him since he was a little kid. There's nothing to tell."

"Not quite," Emmitt says. "Are you two dating?"

Lindsay curls her upper lip. "Gross."

Knowing his daughter, Emmitt takes her comment to mean that she is grossed out by the idea of having a dating talk with him, and not necessarily the idea of dating Troy.

"Well, that's good. Do you like him?" When Lindsay doesn't answer, he pries more. "Lindsay, he's too old to date you, and you're not old enough to date anyone at all."

"C'mon, Dad." Lindsay gives the panel containing the cabin filter a kick. The panel pops open. "Can we just talk about something else?"

"How about we discuss the panel you just knocked out of place?"

Lindsay huffs and struggles to pop the panel in place with her feet.

When talking to his teenage daughter about issues like dating, Emmitt feels like someone attempting to cross a tightrope while balancing spinning plates. One distraction could send the whole act crashing to the ground. Needing to focus, Emmitt turns on the hazard lights and slows the van until he parks it on the side of the road. Dusk is approaching, and the light of the setting sun casts a shadow across Lindsay's face.

"Look, Lindsay. You're in seventh grade. Troy's in the tenth grade, and he'll be driving next year."

Lindsay shakes her head. Emmitt feels the proverbial tightrope shudder beneath him, threatening to bring this conversation to a crashing halt. It would be suicide for him to just come out and forbid her from seeing Troy, even as a friend. So would directly telling her that he doesn't trust the kid because Leo is his father.

Emmitt tries a different approach. "It's just that boys in high school have other intentions."

"What, like sex?" Lindsay questions innocently. "Dad, we're learning about that in health class. Boys in middle school already look at me like that, with those 'other intentions'." Lindsay raises her fingers to tag the last two words with sarcastic air quotes.

With the realization that his daughter knows more about sex than he would care for her to know, Emmitt's focus is gone. The proverbial tightrope breaks, and the conversation crashes and scatters into tiny pieces.

"Fuck," he whispers.

"Dad!" Lindsay shouts and slaps Emmitt on the leg.

"I'm sorry, kiddo. I didn't realize you were so grown up."

"Well, surprise!" She flashes her jazz hands to Emmitt.

"And, for your information, Troy doesn't have those 'intentions'."

Emmitt hits the hazard lights and pulls the van back onto the road. Throughout the rest of the ride home, Emmitt keeps his eyes focused on the road while Lindsay glares out the side window. Once home, Emmitt throws the van in park and gets out. When he makes it to the front steps, he turns.

"Lindsay—"

He spots her sitting, arms crossed, in the front passenger seat. He returns to the car and opens the door.

"Hey, Lindsay, what's wrong?" he asks.

"Daddy," she says. Her voice is low and rough like she had been crying. She looks up at Emmitt. "Can I be a kid a little longer?"

"Sure thing, princess. Anything you want."

Lindsay rises out of the car, and Emmitt pulls her into an embrace and kisses her on the forehead. Together they go inside. Emmitt heads upstairs while Lindsay stays in the dining room to finish her schoolwork.

In his bedroom, Emmitt changes into his security guard uniform. A few years back, he had finally taken the advice of Frank and Willis and picked up a full-time job as a warehouse night guard. This allowed him the opportunity to continue his public charade of being the well-adjusted widower and father. He could see Lindsay off to school every morning, attend her soccer games every afternoon, and even catch dinner with her just before the start of his shift. This was the routine he established every day without interruption until this afternoon when Lindsay decided to have dinner with the team. This he shrugs off as something that a normal teen or preteen would do as she grew up and became more independent from her parents.

Emmitt descends the steps and enters the dining room, where Lindsay is still hard at work. Remaining in the foyer, he watches as she scribbles something on her paper, but then erases it. She slowly writes on the paper with more deliberation. She holds up her paper, squints her eyes, then lays down the paper and continues to write. When he approaches and sits across from her, Lindsay looks up.

"You're leaving already?" She asks, looking at him with eyes that plead for him to stay just a while longer.

"I've got a few moments," says Emmitt. He checks his watch. "What are you working on?"

"A paper for English class. We're supposed to write about a challenge we've had to overcome. But…" She hesitates. "I don't really have anything."

Emmitt takes a deep breath and sits. He knows what he has to say. He just hopes Lindsay will understand.

"Well," he says, "Maybe you could write about how you've dealt with Mom's death."

Lindsay turns away from Emmitt as she shifts in her seat. He sees that this is a lot for her to process, especially since they've managed to skirt around this topic for years, allowing it to build between them a combustion chamber of emotional baggage. Perhaps, he realizes, this isn't the best way to breach this topic.

"I—" Lindsay sniffs. Her eyebrows furrow. "I don't think I can write about that. It's too much."

"I see," Emmitt continues, softening his voice as he does. "You really haven't dealt with this, have you?" Lindsay shakes her head.

"Well," Emmitt says, "neither have I."

He looks at his daughter, whose wide blue eyes glisten in the lamp light. There is always more that he has to say to Lindsay and, he realizes, so much she probably has to say to him.

"Hey, Dad," she says, "you're gonna be late for work."

"Alright, kiddo. But we're going to talk about this," he says and stands.

Lindsay nods and grabs her things.

Exiting the house and walking over to the Burgess's, Emmitt and Lindsay pass through the lawns far away from the shadowy street, lit only by the moon's glow and the porch lights of five houses. These houses belong to people who had the good sense to heed a pamphlet distributed by the neighborhood watch. The pamphlet warned them of a string of robberies that had occurred in the county. *The best deterrent*, the pamphlet said, *is to keep your porch light on.*

On the Burgess's porch, Emmitt kisses Lindsay on the forehead and is glad that she is not too old for this.

"Daddy, before you go, can you promise me something?" Lindsay asks.

"Anything, princess."

"Tell me about how you and Mom met."

Emmitt blinks back the oncoming moisture from his eyes and swallows hard. "Mom already told you that story when you were younger and—"

"But I never heard the story from you." Lindsay's eyes sparkle in the moonlight. "Promise me you'll tell me the story someday."

Emmitt smiles. "I promise."

In the car, Emmitt backs out of his driveway and stops to wave at Lindsay until the interior amber glow of the house envelops her as she heads inside. He drives toward work, away from the shadowy streets and toward the cold light of the warehouse a couple of miles away.

CHAPTER THIRTEEN

December 5, 2005

As daylight begins to creep over the darkness just before dawn, Emmitt drives home. His security guard jacket lies in a rumpled pile on the back seat, and his tie, like the jacket, is wrinkled and hangs loosely from his neck. Fighting sleep, Emmitt takes a sip from a dingy mug containing the cold remains of a pot of coffee brewed halfway through the shift he just finished. Though it would be much easier for him to leave Lindsay in the care of Daniella Burgess during the morning hours, Emmitt's resolve to be more emotionally present in Lindsay's life keeps him showing up even at the most mundane occasions, such as mornings just before school.

Blue and red flashing lights greet Emmitt as he turns down his street. Though his heart races for fear of his daughter's safety, he approaches cautiously when he sees two patrol vehicles parked outside his house. He pulls into the driveway and jumps out when he sees Lindsay still wearing her pajamas and standing on the stoop of the Burgess' house. Daniella stands next to

Lindsay with her arm around her. When Emmitt makes his way toward the Burgess house, Lindsay darts inside.

"Daniella, is she okay?" he asks.

"Yeah," says Daniella. "She's just a little shaken up, Emmitt."

"What's going on?" asks Frank as he approaches everyone. He wears his sheriff uniform and observes Emmitt in his work clothes. "The uniform looks good on you, Emmitt. Maybe I should deputize you."

"Why's that?" asks Emmitt.

"From the 911 call we received, it looks like those robberies we heard about a few months back have finally hit our part of the neighborhood." Frank shakes his head. "Miss Janey just a few doors down had her house broken into."

"Shit." Emmitt glances toward his neighbor's house and his. "Is Miss Janey okay? Did they take anything?"

"Too early to tell, but you might want to take the next few nights off. Hold yourselves up in the house. Keep the rifle loaded just in case. Lindsay can still stay with us if you want."

"I might do that. But I think she'll stay with me. Maybe the time together will be good for us." Emmitt grabs his jacket and lunch bag from the van and heads inside, leaving Frank to tend to police business.

If Emmitt were just another citizen, he would have seriously questioned his friend's competence as sheriff. But he trusts Frank, as he did months ago when he told him his department was closing in on the perpetrators. Even in the last week, Frank confided in him that they've figured out the crooks' patterns. Now, it was only a matter of time until they made a mistake.

In the kitchen, Emmitt is simultaneously preparing Lindsay's lunch and making breakfast they will share together. Though Daniella had extended the offer numerous times to help with Emmitt's morning routine to ease the responsibility of being a single parent, Emmitt had refused.

The front door opens, and cold air seeps in before Lindsay closes the entrance.

"Hey, Dad!" Lindsay cheers. She grins and hugs Emmitt.

"Hey, did you get all your schoolwork done for today?" Emmitt asks, dishing out a small pile of scrambled eggs onto the plates.

"Yep, Aunt Daniella checked it over."

Emmitt places the plates on the table, and Lindsay digs into her helping. She takes a giant bite of toast.

"So, you couldn't wait until I sat down?" Emmitt jokingly asks.

"Sorry, I'm hungry." She places the toast down and waits until Emmitt sits. "Oh, before I forget, can you sign this?" She retrieves a paper slip from her backpack and hands it to Emmitt. "We're going on a field trip. You can check to be a chaperone."

Sitting down and skimming through the sheet, Emmitt frowns. "It says this form is due tomorrow. He looks to Lindsay. "When's the trip?"

"Friday, December 9." She points to the back of the slip. "The date's right there."

Emmitt flips over the paper and sighs. "C'mon, Lindsay. I need more time than that to plan."

"But you're always off on Friday nights." Lindsay pouts.

"Yeah, but I'm never off the overnight shift on Thursday. Do you know how tired I'll be?"

"But—"

"But then again. I was thinking I might take the next few nights off."

"Oh…" Lindsay clutches her backpack.

Emmitt wrinkles his brow. "What's up?"

"It's nothing. I'll talk to Aunt Daniella." She takes a bite of her food and eats slowly.

Emmitt leans closer to Lindsay. "Is it boys? You know you can tell me anything."

At the mention of boys, Lindsay's face reddens. "Aunt

Daniella's got it covered."

"Okay, I'm glad she's got it covered, and you're not 'an item.' Is that the term they're using now?"

Lindsay gives him a blank stare. "Something like that, Dad." She reaches for her orange juice and drinks.

Emmitt sips his coffee thoughtfully, as though its caffeinated nuttiness holds the secret of how to maintain a conversation with his daughter. He places his cup down more forcefully than he intends.

"Hey, maybe we can look at that old photo album. Wouldn't you like to see pics of mom and me?"

Emmitt waits for some response from Lindsay. She clinks, scrapes, and picks at her food. With a smile, she looks up. "Yeah, that'd be cool," Lindsay says.

Emmitt smiles. "Well, let's finish breakfast before it gets cold. I'll see what I can do."

As Emmitt eats the remainder of his breakfast, he notices that Lindsay has hardly touched the rest of her food. For a young lady who claimed to be hungry she doesn't seem that way now.

After finally taking a few small bites, Lindsay looks to Emmitt. She smiles, and her blue eyes seem to sparkle. The sun's rays catch a twinkle at her wrist, drawing Emmitt's attention.

"What do you have there?" he asks. Lindsay's cheeks flush, and she pulls down her cuff.

"It's nothing," she says nonchalantly.

Emmitt tilts his head. "It can't be nothing. I don't remember you ever wearing a bracelet."

"I really like it." She pulls up her sleeve to reveal a silver bracelet. Hanging from the bracelet are tiny silver charms: a heart, an elephant, and a glimmering globe. Emmitt reaches toward the charms and touches the heart.

"They're pretty," he says. "When did you get this bracelet?"

Lindsay rolls her eyes. "Mom got these charms for me. You were away, so you probably don't remember."

Emmitt rises from his seat and rinses his plate at the sink. Though he is almost certain Maggie would have told him about the bracelet and the charms, he decides to lay his suspicions aside for now.

"I'm sorry, princess," he says. "If I'd known, I would have gotten you another charm for your birthday. I'll tell you what, you tell me what brand, and I'll get you one that you can wear to the field trip on Friday."

Glancing at the clock, Lindsay stands. "I think it's Pandora. I don't remember. I gotta catch the bus." She places her dishes in the sink and grabs her bag.

"Hey, I think you're forgetting something!" Emmitt shouts before Lindsay is out the door. He waves the permission slip, then he signs and checks off to be a chaperone. Lindsay jogs over to Emmitt and grabs the paper from him.

"Thank you, Daddy." She gives him a quick hug and bounces toward the door. "Love you!"

"I love you, too, princess. Have a great day."

The door shuts, and Emmitt remains still. Alone in the house, he rubs his weary eyes. He is happy that at least, he and Lindsay have finally talked about losing mom after three years. Three years is a long time to skirt around shared memories and a great deal of stories he has never shared with Lindsay.

Yawning, Emmitt goes upstairs and removes his uniform, draping each piece over his door but stops with a thoughtful smile. Maggie would yell at him for leaving his clothes around the room.

She should still be here, Emmitt thinks to himself.

If she were still here, Maggie would remind him about being there for Lindsay. She'd be right, Emmitt realizes. He needed to be home in the evenings with Lindsay. But changing his shift will have to wait. Right now, he's too tired to think any further on the topic.

He drapes his wrinkled shirt over the door and lays down.

Closing his eyes, a silver bracelet jingling with charms

dwells in his dreams. The clinking and clattering of charms against each other become an incessant pounding that ceases moments before the phone rings.

Emmitt bolts upright, feeling like he hasn't slept at all. For Emmitt, nine thirty-five in the morning means he might as well have stayed awake. He grabs the phone.

"Who is it?" he asks.

"Sorry for waking you, Emmitt," Frank says. "We need to come in."

"Is Lindsay okay?" Emmitt asks.

"Lindsay's fine. Can we come in?"

"Sure, I'll be right down."

Emmitt stands and checks the window. Frank's patrol car is parked out front. Beside the car is a female deputy. She is slim and dark-skinned, wearing an expression that says, *Don't mess with me, I'm fresh out of the academy.*

Pulling on some sweatpants, Emmitt comes down the steps and opens the door. Frank steps in, followed by the deputy.

"Deputy Jeffreys," she says, extending her hand with a bright smile.

Emmitt shakes her hand, which is warm, considering the December chill.

"Sorry, Mr. Wasson," she says as she holds up a slip. "We've got a warrant to search the house."

"For what crime?" Emmitt crosses his arms.

Frank's voice is abrupt. "We need to see Lindsay's room."

Frank moves toward Lindsay's room, but godfather or not, Emmitt steps into his path.

"Is Lindsay involved in something?" Emmitt asks.

"We don't think so," Frank says. "Not directly anyway. We caught one of the perps that claimed he gave out some of the stolen items to several girls in school. One of the girls is Lindsay."

"Shit. What did they give her?"

"Not sure exactly," Frank says. "Did you see her wearing something new recently? A necklace or bracelet?"

"She had a bracelet on this morning that I didn't recognize. Little trinkets dangled from it."

"Charms, you mean?" Deputy Jeffreys asks. "Like from Pandora?"

"Yeah," Emmitt answers. "She claimed Maggie gave it to her. I didn't really believe it, but I didn't tell her that."

Frank chuckles. "Yeah, I wouldn't believe it either. Maggie would have told you. Shit. She probably would have told Daniella, and she would have told me. Did Lindsay wear the bracelet to school?"

Emmitt nods. "I don't think she meant for me to see it, though."

Frank rubs his chin. "She might have other items. We still need to check the room."

"Right this way," Emmitt says.

He leads Frank and Deputy Jeffreys up the steps and into Lindsay's room.

Deputy Jeffreys chuckles. "Quite a mess here. You definitely have a teenage daughter."

Emmitt scratches his head and observes the officers. Frank and Deputy Jeffreys check under the bed, between the mattress, and every other nook they can possibly find. They appear to be looking for something unusual. Emmitt wishes he could assist, but it has been months since he's stepped into Lindsay's room.

"Hey, Frank, do you know who gave her the bracelet?" Emmitt asks.

"Yeah, I do," replies Frank as he continues to search the place. "Miss Janey must've gotten cameras installed after the neighborhood-watch pamphlet came out soon after the break-ins. They filmed the hold thing and helped us catch the kid."

"A kid did this?" Emmitt gulps. "Who was it?"

Frank pauses. "Leo's kid Troy."

"Shit!" Emmitt balls his fists. "If it's okay with you, can I address this with Lindsay this afternoon?"

"Hey, found something," says Deputy Jeffreys. She

holds up a necklace with a locket and opens it. "Unless this family is yours, it's also stolen."

Emmitt and Frank come closer to examine the locket. It contains two pictures: one of a little girl with a toothy grin and long, brown hair, and the other of a man and a woman. The two men shake their heads.

"That's not my family," Emmitt replies, barely above a whisper.

"Okay, we'll take it from here," says Deputy Jeffreys. She places the necklace in an evidence bag. Deputy Jeffreys and Frank search the place for a few more minutes. Finding nothing else, the two officers have Emmitt walk them out.

"Get some rest, Emmitt," Frank says as he leaves with the deputy.

"I don't know if I can," Emmitt replies flatly. He waves to the two officers and gently closes the door.

Emmitt lies down, but he can't sleep. Thinking about Lindsay's betrayal keeps him tossing and turning in bed. He can't believe she lied to him. Hours pass until it's the late morning when Emmitt finally falls asleep.

* * *

Emmitt awakes with a start. Though it's only thirteen minutes after two o'clock in the afternoon, he is wide awake with the understanding that he must have "the talk."

I wish we were having the birds and the bees talk instead, Emmitt thinks. Right now, he would rather talk to Lindsay about boys than about honesty.

With forty-five minutes before Lindsay is due out of school, he decides there is no point in waiting until after the indoor soccer game. He needs to talk to her now. Although his discussion would put a damper on the way she plays, he decides that doesn't matter. She has already betrayed him. He refuses to reward her by letting her play soccer as though nothing has happened.

Though she pretty much carries the team herself, they'd have to suffer without her today.

After a quick clean-up, he throws on khakis and a sweatshirt. On the way out the door, he stuffs a ball cap on his head and stands in the open doorway, testing the temperature and weighing his options. He grabs a light jacket, hops in the van, and heads to the school, racing the afternoon dismissal bell, so he can catch Lindsay before she is able to get on the bus.

Upon his arrival, the buses are already in line, and there is already a convoy of cars — parents waiting to pick up their kids. Bypassing both, Emmitt parks the van in the visitor lot and heads to the front door where he is buzzed in. At the front desk, he shows his ID to one of the secretaries. The secretary stuffs a pair of readers onto her face and studies Emmitt's ID card.

"What can I do for you today, Mr. Wasson?" she asks.

"I'm picking up my daughter Lindsay Wasson." He clears his throat and glances at the clock, uncertain of when the bell rings. He knows he's cutting his time close because the time reads five minutes before three o'clock now.

The secretary punches away at the keys, stops, and leans close to the computer while she tilts her head up. Emmitt wonders why she doesn't just take off her glasses to read the screen.

"Here it is," she says with a sweet patient smile. "Just give me a second as I call down to her room for dismissal." She picks up the phone and presses a few buttons. "Hello, this is the main office. Can you send down —" The bell rings, though she doesn't stop talking. The hallway outside of the main office begins to trickle with middle schoolers. "Oh dear," the secretary says, "I'm not sure if the teacher got the message. You can wait here and see if your daughter meets you."

It takes a great deal for Emmitt to bite back the suggestion that perhaps it may be time for her to retire. Instead, he offers her a tight smile and turns to catch sight of the flood of students passing by the office windows. He watches intently to catch the bobbing of Lindsay's blonde hair pulled back into a ponytail. But to his agitation, a rapid river of brown, black, blonde, auburn, and an occasional red head float by, but none of these belong to his daughter. The bell rings again, and another wave of students pours into the hallway. This too, he watches until it finally dissipates, leaving a few stragglers in its wake.

"Ummm... hey, Dad," Lindsay says.

Shifting his attention, Emmitt sees his daughter standing with her arms crossed by the office entryway. Attempting to mask his feelings of betrayal and disappointment, he gives a faint smile.

"Hey, kiddo," he says. "Thought I'd pick you up today to give us more time together."

"Okay," she says and follows him stiffly out of the school. When they are at the van, she stops. "You're acting weird, Dad."

"How so? Can't a father pick up his daughter after school?"

"Yeah, but you never do that. You usually meet me at soccer."

"Well, get in. I'll drive you."

Lindsay shakes her head. "No, tell me what's up."

Emmitt clears his throat. "I didn't want to do this right now but show me your bracelet."

Lindsay furrows her eyebrows. "Why? You've already seen it."

"I want to see it again." He waits for what seems like an eternity as she glares at him. She places her bag down, pulls up her sleeve, and holds out her arm.

"See." She sarcastically lowers the pitch of her voice. "Are you happy now? Can we just go?"

"No, Lindsay. We can't. It's not yours."

"C'mon, Dad. It is. Mom gave it to me."

"No, Troy gave it to you. It's stolen."

"How did..." she raises the pitch of her voice. "I swear

I didn't know it's stolen."

"Then why was there a necklace hidden in your room?"

"You went into my room. What the hell, Dad?" Emmitt jerks his head back. "Watch your mouth, young lady. I didn't go into your room. Frank and his deputy searched your room because they had a warrant. Did you have anything to do with the robberies?"

"Daddy, No!" Lindsay's eyes begin to glisten. "I was with Aunt Daniella every night. I found out about the robberies from the news, like you. Don't you believe me?"

"What about Troy?"

"What do you mean?" She sniffs, stopping up her tears. With the sleeve of her jacket, she wipes her face and looks at Emmitt. "I haven't seen him since you said not to. I mean, I told him the next day not to come see me."

"How did you get the bracelet and the necklace then?"

"He gave them to me a few months ago. How was I to know?"

"Well, now you do, and you lied to me. Why?"

"I," she pauses and stares at him. "I don't know." Lindsay's tears have faded. She appears defiant. Emmitt clenches his jaw. His neck feels hot, making him second guess why he chose to wear a light jacket with his sweater. He takes a deep breath and counts to three, calming himself down.

"Well, let's go to the station. You can tell them what you do know," Emmitt says.

While Emmitt gets in the van and slams his door shut, Lindsay remains by her door. As she stares through the glass and pouts at him, he realizes that if she were just a few years older, she could very easily run off. Even now, she could do so, but looking at her stiff like an angry gargoyle, it is clear she has no intention of running off. Equally clear, she also has no intention of getting in the car. He rolls down the passenger window.

"Lindsay, get in," he demands. "Let's go."

She shakes her head and says, "Not until you can tell me something."

"What?"

"Are you mad at me?"

Emmitt sighs. "Yes, I'm mad at you, but I still love you, princess. Please get in the car."

Lindsay clicks open the front door and gets in. Driving away from the school, Emmitt plays with the radio dials. The tuner aimlessly lands and rebounds off one station after another.

"What are you looking for?" Lindsay asks.

"Nothing," Emmitt mumbles. He turns off the radio.

Lindsay hesitates. "Did you want to talk about Troy now?"

Emmitt clenches his teeth and grinds out a thought. Troy seemed like he had a good head on his shoulders. He wonders how Troy has been playing games with him and Lindsay.

"Troy's a piece of shit," says Emmitt gruffly.

"No, he's not," retorts Lindsay.

Emmitt glares at Lindsay, shutting her up. He returns his attention to the road until they arrive at the station. Once there, he parks and turns off the ignition.

"You shouldn't cuss, Dad," says Lindsay as she takes off her seat belt.

Emmitt looks at her and smirks. "Neither should you."

Lindsay gives a weak smile. "Daddy, I'm sorry I lied to you. I should've told you about the bracelet and necklace. I was going to give them back to Troy, but...well, you know how that went."

"You know what?" Emmitt's face brightens. "Let's go in and make it right."

Entering the station, they pass by a single room where they see Leo Andreadis and his son Troy seated. With wide eyes, Troy tracks Emmitt and Lindsay as they pass with a single glance and head toward the sheriff's office. In the office, Lindsay hands Frank the bracelet and tells him how she got the bracelet from Troy as a gift. Frank then asks Lindsay a few prompting questions, and she fills in the details.

* * *

Back on the road, Emmitt gives up on the silence between him and his daughter. He pulls over, hits the four-ways, and turns the engine off.

He turns to Lindsay. "How are you feeling?"

"I feel horrible," Lindsay says. She frowns and leans back in her seat. "What's going to happen to Troy?"

Emmitt shrugs. Troy is one of the last people he wants to be thinking about, but he answers his daughter's question anyway. "Detention maybe. He could end up on probation or pay a fine. I'm not sure. It's up to the court now."

Lindsay bites her lip. "Well, I hope he's okay."

Emmitt rakes his hand through his hair. "I wonder what Mom would do right now."

Lindsay blinks twice at Emmitt and looks away. "I try not to think about her."

Emmitt pats Lindsay's shoulder. "To be honest, princess, I think about her every day, and it tears me apart. There are some days I just don't want to do anything at all. I'm sorry."

"For what, Dad?"

He considers telling her everything, but he scoffs. "I'm sorry…for not being there, I guess."

"You were there for me today, and that's something."

"Yeah. I suppose it is." Emmitt drums the steering wheel. Cars pass and honk as though he is blocking traffic. "I feel like I could've been there more for Troy. He used to be a good kid. I don't know what happened."

He and Lindsay look at each other for a long time. Each of them seems to be looking for an answer within each other's eyes. The moment passes, and Emmitt glances at the time.

"Hey, doesn't look like we're going to make it to the game," he says.

"It's okay," Lindsay says.

"You up for some pizza? Maybe we can look at some old photo albums tonight as well."

"Sure."

Although Lindsay remains quiet, Emmitt can tell by the way she relaxes just a little bit that she'll get over being caught. Emmitt and Lindsay are okay for now, though beneath the surface of the emotional calm churns still deeper issues yet unresolved.

After getting pizza and soda, Emmitt and Lindsay pour over a collection of photo albums. Emmitt stops and points to one of the earliest pictures of him and Maggie. He tells Lindsay how he and her mother first met in a bar and how he pulled her away from a group of drunk men that wouldn't leave her alone.

"Mom told me once those guys made her really uncomfortable," replies Lindsay. "Then, you came along." Lindsay beams at Emmitt. "Those guys respected you."

"I guess they did," Emmitt says and watches as Lindsay turns the page of the album in search of another picture to prompt him to tell another story. "Listen. I've got something to tell you. Can you put that away for now?" Emmitt waits for Lindsay to close the album before he tries to find the right words. "So, about your mom... I keep replaying the events that led to the car accident. I can't help but think none of this would've happened if I had been working full-time." He lowers his head. "It's all my fault." Tears sting the corners of Emmitt's eyes.

"Oh, daddy," Lindsay says as her voice cracks. She's on the verge of crying, too. "Mommy wouldn't blame you. She was mad at you, but she really wanted to work, and she loved the job. She told me that. Don't blame yourself."

Though her words bring on a sense of relief for Emmitt, he still can't let himself off that easy by forgetting the part he played in her death.

"Daddy, maybe you can pick the next photo," Lindsay says as she places the album in his lap.

Emmitt reopens the photo album, but the pages seem to blur. The colorful photos of their happy family feel foreign to him. He stops on one of the pages and stares.

"You know, Lindsay," he says, "these next few weeks or maybe even months might be very hard for you."

"Why's that?" she asks.

"Troy might go to trial, and you might have to testify."

"Oh, okay." Lindsay stands up. "I've got some schoolwork to do. Are you okay?"

Emmitt nods, and Lindsay disappears around the corner to head to her room. From downstairs, Emmitt hears her bedroom door shut. Not with a slam, like she is angry. But loud enough to let him know that for the time being she doesn't want to talk about it.

CHAPTER FOURTEEN

January 3, 2006

Emmitt drives Lindsay to court. Within a block or two, Emmitt cannot stand the oppressive silence and daunting discomfort anymore. He needs to set Lindsay at ease.

"Are you okay?" Emmitt asks. "We haven't talked much about Troy since his arrest."

"I don't feel like talking," Lindsay says. She directs her gaze away from him, looking out the passenger window instead.

Emmitt's thoughts return to the countless failed attempts to breach this very topic these last several weeks. Mustering the courage to try a more honest approach, he draws a deep breath before he speaks again.

"Princess, I know this all may be difficult to understand, but it'll all make sense someday." He glances at Lindsay. "Do you remember back when I was away for several months? I think you were six or seven."

"Yeah," Lindsay says. "Mom told me later on that you were an addict. Aunt Daniella told me, too."

"That's right, and you know who saved me?" Lindsay shakes her head, so Emmitt continues. "It was your mom and grandfather. They found out I stashed drugs at the house and had me get help. I hated them, but after a while, I realized that was the best thing they did for me."

With a tilt of her head, Lindsay says, "Cool story, Dad, but what does that have to do with Troy?"

Emmitt sighs. "C'mon, princess, work with me here. I think your testimony will help Troy, just like Mom and your grandfather helped me. Troy may even thank you for it later."

Lindsay shakes her head. "I doubt that. He won't ever see me again."

Pulling into the courthouse parking lot, Emmitt resists the urge to press further. He recalls Dr. Phillips' advice:

Although she won't express it, she will come around when she is ready and appreciate you for being present and honest.

Emmitt keeps the doctor's words in mind as Lindsay mentally and emotionally prepares to testify.

"I guess we should go in," Lindsay mumbles.

Lindsay gets out of the van and slams the door shut behind her. Without waiting for Emmitt, she marches toward the courthouse. Hopping out of the van, Emmitt catches up to her.

Just outside the doors of the courthouse, Lindsay stops and turns to him. "Dad, do you really think Troy won't hate me?"

"Umm…" Emmitt pauses, and answers with as much honesty as possible. "I really don't know, princess. I guess time will tell."

Saying nothing more on the matter, Lindsay pushes the doors open, and Emmitt follows her inside. He offers up a silent prayer for strength for his daughter. Then, recalling his own need for forgiveness for the hurt he caused his own family; he offers up a halfhearted prayer of forgiveness for Troy. In this way, he is like Jonah refusing his call to preach to the Ninevites for fear they will turn from their wickedness and enjoy God's mercy.

In his heart of hearts, he prays he never sees the kid again.

* * *

During the trial, the prosecuting attorney brings to discovery that at only age sixteen, Troy had managed to put together quite an operation, stockpiling goods worth a combined total of over ten thousand dollars. When this comes to light, Emmitt cannot help but turn his attention toward Troy, who, though sullen in his appearance, manages to cast an arrogant glare around the room. When Troy locks eyes with Emmitt, Troy's facial expression softens for a moment then transforms into a sneer. Emmitt seethes within at the knowledge that this kid had been seeking to corrupt his daughter behind his back for months and possibly for years without his knowledge.

When Lindsay takes the stand, Emmitt can see she is more than a little nervous. As Lindsay speaks, Emmitt's heart wrenches. She mentions how long she has known Troy and his extracurricular activities. First, she notes his vandalism, then talks about how he began to steal school supplies from teachers. As she goes on with this little history, she brings up more recent occurrences. She talks about how he visited her almost every night for months. Some nights Troy would give her a new gift, like a necklace. Other nights he would have something else for her, but she would refuse.

"Why would you refuse?" the prosecuting attorney asks.

"I thought," Lindsay says as she leans into the mic, "I thought they might be stolen gifts."

"Why did you think this?"

Lindsay pauses for a moment. "Some of them looked like jewelry that I saw some of my neighbors wearing."

"Why didn't you report this?"

Lindsay shrugs. "I don't know. I guess I had hoped

they weren't stolen."

When the prosecuting attorney sits, the defense attorney approaches the stand. He is slow and deliberate, like a hungry tiger on the prowl.

"Where was your father?" the defense attorney asks as he glances first at the jury, and then at Emmitt.

"He was at work," Lindsay says.

"So, he left you home alone, then?"

"No, I would stay with our neighbors Frank and Daniella Burgess. They're my godparents."

"Is this Frank Burgess the Sheriff?" Lindsay nods, and the defense attorney continues. "So, you had items you believed were stolen in your possession, and you didn't think to tell your godfather, Sheriff Burgess?"

When Lindsay goes to speak, the prosecuting attorney raises an objection, which the judge sustains.

"Did Troy meet with you at Sheriff Burgess's house or your house?" asks the defense attorney.

Lindsay shifts in her seat, and so does Emmitt.

"He met me at my house," Lindsay says. She makes eye contact with Emmitt as though speaking directly to him. "I would sneak out, and we would meet at my house where we would..." Lindsay trails off as tears well up in her eyes.

"Where you would what?" asks the defense attorney. "Were you and Troy in a sexual relationship?"

"Objection," the prosecuting attorney calls. "The witness is not on trial, and the nature of their relationship has no bearing on Troy's guilt or innocence."

The judge sustains the objection, and the defense attorney finishes with a few more questions, none of which Emmitt listens to. Embarrassment before the court fuels his anger at Troy, his daughter for sneaking about, and himself. The defense attorney ceases his questioning, and the judge dismisses Lindsay from the stand.

Emmitt watches as Lindsay is red with shame and

avoids eye contact with him. She steps off the witness stand and makes her way down the aisle. Between herself and Emmitt, Lindsay sits to create a chasm wide enough to cool his anger. He realizes he cannot let his anger fall upon his own daughter. Though she doesn't move, her eyes remain downcast as though gazing into an abyss. Emmitt shifts closer to her and closes the gap. He wraps his arm around her, pulling her to himself and kissing her on the forehead.

"I love you, princess," Emmitt says. "You did good."

In his arm, Lindsay cries, which creates a slight disturbance in the courtroom. The judge raps his gavel. Emmitt nudges Lindsay up, and they walk toward the exit. Before exiting, Emmitt glances behind him, locking eyes with Troy once again. Troy smirks, fueling the smoldering coals within Emmitt's heart until the heat reignites the flame of anger as Emmitt exits with Lindsay.

* * *

That evening Emmitt and Lindsay peck at their meal in silence. Emmitt occasionally glances at her, wondering what happened between her and Troy for what must have been countless nights over several months. Lindsay looks up.

"Daddy," she says in a barely audible whisper. "It's not what you think. We kissed and made out. That's all." Emmitt takes a deep breath, offering a silent prayer of thanks.

"Even if it were more than that, it wouldn't change the way I see you," Emmitt says. "You'll always be my daughter. I'll always love you."

"Thanks, Dad," Lindsay says. She gets up from the table. "I'm tired." Leaving Emmitt alone to clean up, Lindsay heads upstairs.

CHAPTER FIFTEEN

January 4, 2006

The next morning, the attorneys deliver their closing arguments, and the jury deliberates. An hour passes and the jury returns with a guilty verdict for several accounts of felony theft. The jury sentences Troy to five years in juvenile detention with the opportunity for parole in two.

Emmitt can't help being overjoyed at this outcome as it will put Troy out of Lindsay's purview for the time being. He also hopes Troy will be out of her mind forever as a result. Lindsay, however, is pissed. When they return home, she locks herself in her room and cries.

For the next week, Lindsay closes herself off to Emmitt. Though he persists in trying to connect with his daughter while taking her to her games and dropping her off at school and social events, none of the time together gives way to honest dialogue between Emmitt and Lindsay. Finally, they find themselves once again in session with Dr. Phillips.

"He hates Troy," Lindsay says.

Dr. Phillips waits for more, glancing at Emmitt.

Emmitt realizes he has been impatiently shaking his leg and wanting to defend himself. He ceases the shaking and listens.

"I mean," Lindsay continues. "I don't think he hates Troy. Troy was kind of a butt. But I'd like to go see him while he's in the detention center. Everyone needs forgiveness."

Emmitt feels as though Lindsay has intentionally directed this last statement toward him.

"I just don't know if I can handle that right now," Emmitt says, recalling the snide and arrogant way in which Troy looked at him as he led Lindsay out of the courtroom.

"Why is that?" Dr. Phillips asks.

"I guess," Emmitt begins, "because everyone has to come to the point of accepting their responsibility for messing in other people's lives."

Dr. Phillips gives a slight nod. "Like the way you have to accept feeling like you are to blame for your wife's death?"

"Yes," Emmitt says. He turns his attention to Lindsay. "I'm sorry, Lindsay. I just think we're at very different places. I don't think Troy is willing to own up to the way he has tampered with your life. I don't think he even cares."

"Let's focus this on you two," Dr. Phillips says. "Lindsay, what did you think when you first heard your dad talk about how he felt guilty for your mom's death?"

"I guess I was shocked," says Lindsay. "I mean, I didn't really know what to think. I hated knowing this, especially right before I had to testify against Troy."

"Why's that?" Dr. Phillips asks.

"Because I kept thinking that if my dad had made a different decision, then maybe this thing with Troy wouldn't have happened."

"Oh, Lindsay," Dr. Phillips says. "Everyone makes their own decisions, including you. Now, what decision are you going to make?"

Lindsay looks at Emmitt. "I guess if you decide not to take me to see Troy, it's fine."

"Does this mean we're on speaking terms again?" Emmitt asks hopefully.

"Sure," she says.

After this session, they begin to talk again at home, and having their usual after game outings continue. However, both tiptoe around the topic of seeing Troy. Emmitt refuses to bring it up and Lindsay occasionally asks, but he refuses to even acknowledge the question.

Months pass, and the topic revises itself with the added distraction of Leo Andreadis who, with very few others to talk to in Troy's absence, comes around often, and mostly uninvited. Every time he does, Lindsay asks how Troy is doing. Whenever Leo talks about Troy, Lindsay throws Emmitt an icy glare and she storms upstairs, where she stays for the remainder of the night until it is time for Emmitt to go to work. This routine continues for six months until Emmitt is fed up. One day Emmitt finally tells Leo he can't visit anymore or talk about Troy around his daughter. Leo complies, and Emmitt is content for a moment.

CHAPTER SIXTEEN

April 8, 2008

A fluorescent bulb flickers above the desk in which Emmitt sits as he looks over Lindsay's grades. Her report card came in the afternoon mail just before he made his way out the door of the house to see Lindsay at one of her games. When he had picked up the mail, he had torn it open and briefly glanced at it without a close examination. Now, in the middle of his shift when all is quiet, he is looking at the report card with greater intensity.

Emmitt can see from the first and second quarters that Lindsay had done well. In fact, she had been nearly a straight A student with a single B in Science to mar her record. Yet, looking at the report card more closely, the third quarter report tells a much different story. In her core classes, Lindsay holds a C, while in her electives, she is barely holding a D. On top of that, her attendance record shows that in some classes, she has missed almost twenty days. Folding the report card carefully and stuffing it into his breast pocket, Emmitt cannot help but feel that something else beyond the workload is taking place. He only hopes he doesn't blow up at her when he confronts her about these grades and her attendance.

With the report secured, Emmitt checks the time. It is nearly five o'clock in the morning, and time to do another round. He glances at the black and white grainy glow of closed-circuit televisions scrolling past images of the vacant warehouse. When the feed portrays the offices, Emmitt sees the movement of the only other person in the building, a twenty-something-fresh-out-of-college I.T. guy named Sam. Rarely does Emmitt have an occasion to talk with Sam, nor does he make an effort to do so. The night watch carries with it a soothing stillness that Emmitt could barely stand when he first took on this job, and now he will do nothing to disturb its sacredness. Therefore, he doesn't bother to call the Burgesses' house, where Lindsay still stays the night while he is at work. Emmitt figures it is best to mull over and even practice his approach regarding her grades, rather than call her right away.

Emmitt stretches, picks up his coffee mug, and begins his hourly rounds of the building. He stops at the warehouse's cafe and fills up on coffee, the only companion he would ever need during his rounds. As with the previous hours, the warehouse is clear, all doors are locked, and he returns to his desk to log his hourly account. When he puts pen to paper, an alarm from the CCTVs begins to buzz. Pressing a few buttons on the console takes Emmitt to a digital map on one of the screens. On the digital map, a circle marking out the alarm points, flashes red.

Cursing, Emmitt grabs the radio and retraces the steps he took through the warehouses until he finds Sam. "Excuse me," Emmitt says. But when he gets no reply, Emmitt knocks on the cubicle wall and the kid looks up, eyes wide with surprise like he'd been caught doing something he knows he shouldn't be doing. Sam removes his earbuds and nods.

"Hey," Emmitt says, then points behind him. "Any

idea what's behind those doors? There's an alarm going off in there."

"Oh, that's not good," Sam says. "That's the electrical room. Our network operates from within. What's up?"

"Not sure. Maybe you can help me locate the source of the alarm."

With Sam a pace or two behind him, Emmitt strides rapidly toward the door. The door opens to the sound of gushing water. Inside, a gaping hole of brick and concrete pours forth a waterfall onto the floor. He stands there, just outside the door, struck by the notion that there is only a need for a security guard in the event of an emergency. Otherwise, they are just a warm body keeping watch over a silent, uneventful night. Of course, a catastrophe would strike during his night shift.

"We've gotta reroute the water!" shouts Sam. He moves forward, but Emmitt stops him.

"No, Sam," Emmitt states as he steps onto the little bit of dry concrete still in the room. "You've gotta get out of the water before you get hurt."

Emmitt steps back onto the carpet and Sam follows him just before the growing puddle upon the concrete floor reaches their feet. The two round the corner of the exterior of the room until they reach a hallway leading to a rear emergency exit door. Water is already beginning to flow beneath the door and soak the carpet.

"Sam, call your supervisor and get out of the building!" shouts Emmitt. Sam nods and leaves.

Emmitt charges away from the oncoming water and past the cubicles that are now within just a few feet of the water that has made its way out of the electrical room. Running toward the security office, Emmitt dials the number for Ron, his supervisor, who is retired and just crankily passing his time as a warehouse guard. Getting no answer, Emmitt leaves a calm message in which he tells Ron that water is rushing into the building and flooding the complex. He does the same for the building manager, who also doesn't pick up. Stepping outside, Emmitt waits and watches the front entrance of the building until Sam appears, jogs down the steps, and plants himself right next to Emmitt. Sam pulls out a cigarette and offers him one. Emmitt declines. Within a few minutes, Emmitt receives a call back from his supervisor and building manager.

Fifteen minutes pass before fire trucks wail onto the scene. Following close behind the trucks are the building manager, the company CEO, and several other apparently important and sour people who would much rather be home in bed than here on site. They rush into the building, and Emmitt remains outside, watching the drama unfold. As he watches, he wishes for just two things: popcorn and his bed. With his shift over in less than half an hour, he hopes this doesn't hold him up too long. By this time, Lindsay Jane should be waking up for school, and he does not want to miss another morning with her, even if it may be almost as dramatic as what he is watching now.

Since entering high school, Lindsay has become close friends with Ashley. Although Ashley is a junior while Lindsay is a freshman, the two get along well. The last time Emmitt had missed Lindsay because Ashley had picked her up to study for an exam. As of late, they have been spending so much time together. Emmitt must make the most of his time with Lindsay, so breakfast has become precious. He needs to get home soon.

"Hey, Sam, can I borrow your cell phone?" Emmitt asks.

Sam hands him the phone, and Emmitt dials Frank and Daniella's number. It rings twice before Daniella answers.

"Heya, Emmitt," she says.

"Hey, is Lindsay up?" he asks.

"Actually, she left already."

"Did Ashley pick her up?"

"I'm not sure. I recall her saying something last night about leaving early in the morning to study."

Unable to recall whether Lindsay had mentioned this to him as well, Emmitt glances around. He sees the building is spewing forth flood waters in the way a creek bed may do during heavy rain. Or the way Lindsay's teenage years seem to be spewing forth sudden and erratic behavior such as leaving without telling anyone.

"Hey, I've gotta go. I'll be home late anyway."

"Is there trouble at work?"

"Yeah, you can say that. I'll fill you in later, okay?"

He hangs up and watches debris in the form of light office furniture and stray papers flow down the steps of the building and land upon the blacktop as the building's creek spreads and creates a shallow lake over the parking lot. This he surveys with an awe that only increases when the firemen and the company managers exit the building while treading knee-deep in water. All are, at least, temporarily lost in the damaging effects of the water for this business and its stakeholders, and Emmitt hopes that his relationship with Lindsay is not lost.

The men approach Ron, Emmitt's supervisor, who speaks with them for a moment. As Ron speaks, he points to Emmitt, and the men glance his way, then return their attention to Ron. They exchange a few more words, and the managers walk away, leaving Ron by himself.

"This sure is a shit storm," says Ron as he approaches Emmitt. "How'd you keep it together?"

"It's what I was trained for," Emmitt says.

Ron nods and lights a cigarette. "Well, your shift's over. You can stay for O.T., or you can head off. Just fill out an incident report before you do."

What should only take a few minutes, takes Emmitt ten times as long as he documents the details of the incident as he experienced it, making certain to remain objective. This takes a few pages of writing, eating into over a half hour of time after his shift before finally handing Ron the incident report. Ron flips through it and nods.

"You take care of yourself," says Ron. "I'll be calling you later with an adjusted schedule."

Back in the car and turning the key, Emmitt grins. There is no way Lindsay would ever believe this story. Driving away, he rehearses and seeks ways to embellish the drama, incident by incident, so that he can retell it to his daughter when he meets her tonight after soccer practice for dinner.

Pulling into his driveway, Emmitt feels the exhaustion setting in. He waves to Daniella then passes through their neighboring front yards until he is looking up at her. Daniella holds a steaming cup of coffee in both her hands. Though he called her over an hour and a half ago, she is still dressed in a worn robe as though she has just woken up. *Retirement must be nice.*

"Crazy night at work, huh, Emmitt?" Daniella asks.

Emmitt nods and gives her the unembellished and abridged version of the night's event.

Daniella shakes her head. "That's sure some story. You think you're going to be in the papers?"

"No, I don't think so. Did you catch what exam Lindsay was studying for?"

Daniella takes a sip of coffee, squints, and sucks in her upper lip as though on the brink of espousing some profound revelation about the brew, which she swallows and sips again.

"Yes, she mentioned a biology exam," says Daniella. "In fact, Ashley popped on by for a bit last night. After she left, Lindsay said she would be leaving early for a study group."

"Oh, that reminds me." Emmitt pulls out Lindsay's report card from his breast pocket, unfolds it, and hands it to Daniella. "For someone who's been studying so much, you'd think her grades would be better."

There is a stretch of silence as Daniella reads over the report card, which she hands back to Emmitt. "These grades and absences aren't like Lindsay."

"I'm gonna call the school later and find out why I was never notified until the report card."

After wishing Daniella a good day, Emmitt crosses the lawn and goes into his house. He tosses his keys in a jar just inside the door and walks to the kitchen. As he does so, he hears creaking upstairs that makes him freeze. The noise rhythmically reverberates through the floorboards. For a moment, the rhythm stops. Then, it starts again until it crescendos to another rest. Emmitt's heartbeat quickens. His breath grows shallow, and his stomach turns. He darts upstairs to find the source of the noise coming from within his daughter's bedroom.

At the door of her bedroom, Emmitt listens and lifts his hand into a fist to knock.

"Troy, stop!" Lindsay shouts in her room.

In response, the steady rhythm continues. Emmitt grabs the doorknob and throws open the door. In the same instant, Troy yanks his jeans up, covering his bare bottom, and turns toward Emmitt.

"What the fuck?" Troy asks.

Emmitt grabs Troy in a headlock while Lindsay attempts to get him out of it.

"No, Daddy, don't hurt him!" she yells.

Emmitt ignores Lindsay's wishes. Normally, he'd do anything for his daughter, but not this time. Right now, he wants Troy out of his house and out of his life.

In one swift motion, Emmitt drags Troy down the hallway and steps before he tosses him down the last few. Troy stumbles and catches himself on a railing halfway down the steps and lands on his butt. Emmitt quickly closes the distance between himself and Troy. He lifts him to his feet and tosses him toward the front door. Troy crumples to the floor, and Emmitt crouches to pull him up.

"Daddy, you can't do this!" cries Lindsay.

Emmitt looks up. Lindsay is standing on the landing. Her legs are bare from just above the middle of her thighs down to her feet. She wears a thin, dingy white revealing t-shirt.

"Lindsay, get back to your room and get dressed!" Emmitt yells.

"I hate you," she says through gritted teeth.

"You're gonna hate me even more if you don't get to your room." He makes like he is about to charge up the steps.

This gets her moving. She disappears around the corner. Her footsteps pound down the hallway and cease with the slamming of her door.

By Emmitt's feet, Troy groans and begins to sit up. When he attempts to rise to his feet, Emmitt steps toward him, and Troy returns to his upright, but seated position.

"Dude, what the fuck?" asks Troy as he winces. "You know I can sue you, right?"

"And we can press charges for rape," Emmitt says coldly.

"C'mon, man. It wasn't like that. Lin wanted it."

"Get the fuck out of my house, Troy."

"Not until I get my shirt."

There is a pounding at the door.

"Emmitt, it's Deputy Jeffreys," replies the officer. "Is everything all right?"

"No, can you come in here? The spare key is under the mat," Emmitt says.

Deputy Jeffreys enters the house.

"That's quite a response time, deputy," Emmitt says.

"Yeah," says Deputy Jeffreys, "I was just in the neighborhood when..." She pauses as her eyes land upon Troy. "Look who you've got here." She shakes her head slowly with a *tsk*.

"Seems Troy's time in juvenile detention didn't teach him anything," Emmitt says. "I caught him with his pants down in Lindsay's room."

"Is she okay?"

Emmitt scratches his head. "I don't know."

"Tell you what?" Deputy Jeffreys grabs Troy. "I've got

Troy. You go ahead and check on your daughter. Sheriff Burgess'll be along in ten, maybe fifteen minutes."

Emmitt nods, and his trek up the steps seems endless as he replays the events that occurred. Troy has busted back into Lindsay's life, leaving in his path the rubble of what remains of his relationship with his daughter. Even worse, if a handbook came with fatherhood, Emmitt is certain nothing would be in there on what to do when you catch your daughter and a boy having sex, especially when your daughter is a minor and the boy is an adult. But one thing is for certain, as he told Lindsay a long while back, nothing can ever change the fact that she is his daughter. He can only hope that he is not too late to reroute Troy's destructive path and repair the damage.

Emmitt knocks on Lindsay's door and waits. He knocks again, and there is no answer. "Lindsay, I'm coming in," he calls and cautiously turns the knob. He hopes she's dressed now and glad to see him. After all, he did save her, or so he thinks.

Stepping into the room, he sees that the room is silent, and the windows are shut. There is no way she could have possibly gotten out and shut the windows on her own. But he sees that her bathroom door is shut, too. Maybe she couldn't hear him when he knocked. He walks over to the door and knocks.

"Lindsay, princess, please open the door," pleads Emmitt.

Again, there is no answer. There isn't even the tell-tale sign of her presence in the room. Emmitt rushes past the steps and sees the deputy is on her way upstairs.

"Deputy Jeffreys, can you please help?" asks Emmitt in a panic. "Lindsay's locked herself in her bathroom. She's not answering!"

"Okay, slow down," Deputy Jeffreys says. "If you have a key, we can open the door. If not, we can bust it down."

"I've got a key. It's in my bedroom. I'll go get it." As

he leaves the bedroom, he hears Deputy Jeffreys continue to knock on the bathroom door.

Once in his bedroom, Emmitt rummages through a drawer filled with some of Maggie's jewelry, a tie clip, and several plastic collars until he finds a ring of keys. With keys in hand, he runs down the hallway and into Lindsay's bedroom.

"You got them," Deputy Jeffreys says and steps to give Emmitt room to unlock the door.

"You hear that, Lindsay," Emmitt says. "We're opening the door."

He fumbles with the unfamiliar keys. Since owning the house, Emmitt can only recall one other time when he used these keys, and this was to unlock the bathroom door down the hall, the one Lindsay used to use when she was younger. At the time, she had accidentally locked herself in and couldn't figure out how to open the door again. Emmitt and Maggie had panicked then as they listened to her crying on the other side of the door. Now, with the same keys in hand, Emmitt is panicking again, especially since there is no sound from the other side. His heart begins to race, and his breathing becomes rapid. He can't imagine what Lindsay must be doing to herself on the other side of the door.

The door swings open halfway and comes to a stop. Emmitt steps in and sees Lindsay propped against the bathtub in the same t-shirt he told her to change. Her eyes are glazed over as she stares at the wall.

"Lindsay!" Emmitt screams and kneels by her side.

From behind him, he hears Deputy Jeffreys call an ambulance on the radio, while he remains inside, holding her tightly.

"Oh, Lindsay," he whispers. "What have you done?"

CHAPTER SEVENTEEN

April 9, 2008

Twenty-four sleepless hours pass. Emmitt's routine consists of pacing, sitting and praying. His vigil is made only slightly more bearable by the silent company of the presence of Frank and Daniella Burgess and Lindsay's teammate Ashley Robertson and her father. They do the same as Emmitt, sending up prayers and wrapping an arm around him for support. Though Emmitt receives the support, even sharing stories of joyful memories of times when he and his family were whole, he is all alone when the noise dies down, leaving him to listen to the steady beeping of Lindsay's heart monitor.

"Lindsay, please come back to me, princess," Emmitt whispers. "I don't know what drove you to this point. Was it me? Did I say or do something that pushed you over the edge?"

He looks upon Lindsay's face. It is peaceful and still bears traces of the childlike innocence that it once possessed. He takes her hand in his and waits as though for an answer. Yet her eyes remain closed, and her hand does not return his grasp. Letting go, he stands and kisses Lindsay on the forehead.

"I'll be back," he says.

Aimless roaming allows Emmitt time to himself. Being around, so many people gave him so little time to process how the penetrating presence of Troy Andreadis entered Lindsay's life. More importantly, how it came to be that Lindsay would overdose on heroin. Having only experienced an addiction to painkillers himself, he concludes that somehow Lindsay's relationship with Troy must be connected to heroin.

Emmitt's aimlessness gains a new sense of purpose: to find a pay phone on which he can call Frank Burgess. Emmitt recalls how Lindsay has mentioned to him to get a cell phone. She even went on to present him with a hundred and one reasons why having a cell phone is so important. Aside from emergencies and the argument that she is the only one without a cell phone, Lindsay has told Emmitt he could talk more with her while he was at work. Just last week Lindsay had begged Emmitt to get her a cell phone. She even brought him a brochure with some sort of family plan deal, yet he had tossed the brochure to the side. He didn't think he needed a cell phone, until now. Emmitt steps up to the nearest hospital counter, where the receptionist sits.

"Excuse me, ma'am, where's your nearest public phone?" he asks.

"Do you mean a payphone?" the woman asks. "They took those out several years ago because no one used them."

"I need to make a phone call, but I don't have a cell phone."

"If you want, you can use the office line really quick." She hands him the receiver. Emmitt thanks the woman and rattles off Frank's number, which she punches in.

"Hello, this is Sheriff Burgess," says Frank.

"Frank, it's me," replies Emmitt. "I'm still at the hospital with Lindsay."

"How is she?"

110

"Resting and stable. She hasn't woken up, yet. But doctors say she will recover just fine. There's no internal damage."

"That's good to hear, but I suspect that's not the only reason for the call."

"No, it's not. I was wondering about what's going to happen to Troy."

"Provided Lindsay recovers and testifies, he'll probably face rape charges. Even if she doesn't testify, we can make a case against him anyway."

"And what about Lindsay?"

"She should be fine, especially if we can connect the needle we found next to her with him. Lab's processing it right now."

"What do you mean she should be fine?"

"I'll handle it. You just take care of Lindsay."

Emmitt returns the phone to the attendant on duty, and she smiles.

Emmitt turns, and his thoughts brood with possibilities that range from more stolen items to the idea of selling them to fund an addiction. No longer wandering, Emmitt takes the shortest route to Lindsay's room and finds a nurse, checking her vitals.

"Your daughter's doing fine," says the nurse with a smile.

"Is she up yet?" Emmitt asks.

The nurse's smile fades, and she shakes her head. "No, I'm sorry, but we'll let you know as soon as she does." She inches closer to Emmitt. "When did you last sleep, sir?"

Emmitt shrugs. "Maybe Monday afternoon."

"Well, it's Wednesday afternoon now. You look like you're going to crash."

Emmitt sighs and sits down. "Well, I'll get some shut eye here, if that's okay."

The nurse leaves, and Emmitt glances at Lindsay. He wonders what else has happened in Lindsay's room. He remembers that she had told Troy to stop, but he's unsure what she meant. Also, Emmitt finds that the more he thinks about what happened in Lindsay's room, the tougher it will be for him to sleep. Instead of worrying himself, he pulls open the drawer of the nightstand beside her bed and smiles when he finds a Bible upon which is the familiar two handled pitcher and torch of the Gideons.

He flips through the Bible randomly. As a Catholic, he never really learned to navigate through the Bible. As one who has been nominal at best, he cannot even remember the last time he attended church. Not since his own stint with rehab. Somewhere in the recesses of his memory, he recalls the horrors experienced by God's people as a result of their disobedience. Perhaps, he thinks, this tragedy is the logical result of faithlessness.

The pages of the Bible cease in their turning, and Emmitt's eyes lock onto the page before him. He reads aloud:

"Because he has set his love upon Me, therefore I will deliver him; I will set him on high because he has known My name. He shall call upon Me, and I will answer him; I will be with him in trouble; I will deliver him and honor him. With long life, I will satisfy him and show him My salvation."

Two more times, he reads this passage aloud, and two more times, he looks to Lindsay until he closes the book. He puts the Bible away and leaves the room.

His walking is fast. Occasionally, he maneuvers around a few nurses and food service workers who cut him off without seeing him. Emmitt is looking up as he walks, shifting his eyes until he lands upon a sign that reads "Chapel." He heads down this hallway until he comes to a great room with simple wooden icons marking each Station of the Cross. The room is dimly lit, and the faint familiar scent of myrrh permeates the atmosphere. To the right of the altar, a few votive candles are lit before an icon of The Divine Mercy. In a few short paces, for the chapel is small, Emmitt approaches the icon and bows. Then he pulls a wooden stick from a tray of sand, lights the burnt end of the stick with the flame of one of the candles, and shields this new flame as he lowers it to light a new candle. He extinguishes the flame of the stick by stuffing it back into the sand. Gazing at the image of Christ before him, he kneels

He closes his eyes and takes a deep breath. He visualizes Lindsay alone in her hospital bed, unconscious. Tears come to Emmitt's eyes and slowly roll down his cheeks. His lips are incapable of putting to words his deepest desire to speak to Lindsay and his even deeper need for God's mercy to bring Lindsay and himself the healing they so desperately need. He stands, pulls out a few bills from his wallet and inserts these into a slot, then bows before the image and leaves with the uncertainty that God will even understand if he has not actually voiced a prayer.

Emmitt returns to Lindsay's room. Seeing no apparent change in her, he kisses her on the forehead.

"Lindsay, I want you to know that no matter what, I'm not leaving," whispers Emmitt. "I love you, princess." He gazes at Lindsay, willing her to wake until the heaviness of his own eyes forces him to sleep.

CHAPTER EIGHTEEN

April 10, 2008

"Daddy," Lindsay's voice calls. Her voice is muffled, like she is speaking through a pillow or some heavy blankets. "Daddy, wake up."

Emmitt feels the warmth of her hands upon his shoulders. Lindsay shakes him gently until he finally opens his eyes.

It is dark, but the light of a lamp in the room glows on Lindsay's face. She sits up in her bed, looking at him with wide eyes and furrowed brow. Emmitt shifts in his chair, and layers of blankets fall from his chest and crumple upon his lap.

"You were shivering," says Lindsay, "so I asked the nurse for more blankets."

"Thank you," Emmitt says. "When did you wake up?"

Lindsay shrugs. "Not too long ago. Here, I saved you the jello."

Emmitt takes the spoon and jello cup. He peels back the foil and eats the whole cup.

"Thank you, princess," says Emmitt. "I guess I was hungrier than I thought. How long was I asleep?"

"I think about twelve hours," Lindsay says. "The nurse said she last saw you awake around one o'clock in the afternoon. It's two in the morning right now."

"Oh." Emmitt is surprised by Lindsay's chattiness. For a girl who has just awoken from an overdose, she is quite lively. Even though she is like this normally, he would have expected her to be less talkative. Even worse, shivering and sweaty the way addicts suffering from withdrawal tend to be. Maybe God did indeed understand exactly what he needed.

"Daddy, I'm really sorry," she says. Her voice trembles, though she is far from being on the verge of sobbing.

Nonetheless, Emmitt stands, lowers the metal rail on her bed, and sits beside her.

"I forgive you, princess. You really gave me a scare."

"You did, too."

"What do you mean?"

"I thought you were going to kill Troy."

In the heat of the moment days ago, it hadn't occurred to Emmitt how he must have looked to his own daughter. Looking back, the image of Troy's face terrified and angry, must have been close to what his daughter felt as well.

"I'm sorry, Lindsay," says Emmitt. "I'm your father. I'm not sure how I should've reacted when I heard you yelling at Troy to stop. Then, when I saw you two together..."

He sees Lindsay divert her eyes. "Can we not talk about that right now, please?"

"Okay, but can I ask you something?"

"Umm...sure."

He waits until Lindsay nods, but he can tell by her hesitation that even this is something she may not want to talk about.

"Something was retrieved from your bedroom and filed as evidence," says Emmitt. "Any idea what that was?"

Lindsay frowns and bites her lip. "They were needles, Dad. Troy brought them."

"How long have you been using?"

She closes her eyes, shutting herself off from Emmitt. An answer is not necessary, though. Emmitt pulls out Lindsay's third quarter grade report and guesses that her drug use has been going on for weeks, if not months. He folds the grade report up and slides it back into his shirt pocket, deciding this conversation is one that will happen some other time.

"Hey, kiddo," Emmitt says and leans in, giving Lindsay a kiss on the cheek. She turns away with a groan and wipes the moisture away with her blanket. "I love you, you know that, right?"

Lindsay opens her eyes. A slight smile is upon her face. "I know, daddy. I love you, too."

"Get some rest," he says and pulls her blankets close to her, tucking her in. As he does, his heart fills with fear that Lindsay has already succumbed to an irreversible addiction. Though the tell-tale signs upon the skin are not currently present, her soul has already been ripped open, and the demon of addiction could already have taken up residence.

Emmitt sits. He shivers and pulls his own blankets close to him, but the blankets do nothing to ease the chill of anger that overcomes him. Whatever happens, he cannot let Troy come close to Lindsay again.

CHAPTER NINETEEN

June 3, 2008

Emmitt sits outside Lindsay's high school, waiting for her dismissal. Ever since her release from the hospital, Emmitt has closely monitored Lindsay's whereabouts. With his schedule adjusted at work, he has been able to drop Lindsay off at school in the morning, put his time in at work, and meet her at four-thirty in the afternoon on school days. Normally, school is out at two-thirty in the afternoon, but Lindsay is the exception. The teachers have allowed her to make up her assignments, so she stays after to complete them. Unfortunately, Lindsay couldn't return to the soccer team this season, but Emmitt thinks that choice is for the best.

Emmitt checks his watch. It's four-thirty. Lindsay should be exiting the school building any moment.

The phone rings.

Getting a phone is another change that Emmitt reluctantly embraced. Now that he has a phone, he can stay in touch with those closest to him. He believes the mishap between Lindsay and Troy could have been avoided, but there's nothing he can do about it now. A few months ago, Lindsay refused to testify against Troy, but the evidence against him was sufficient. Troy has received one year in prison for statutory rape and another year for possession of drugs, with zero contact with Lindsay, to Emmitt's relief.

The phone rings again. Emmitt picks it up.

"Hey, Dad, it's me," Lindsay says.

"What's going on?" Emmitt asks frantically. "Are you coming out?"

"Yeah, I'll be out in a few. My teacher has me finishing a unit test."

"Okay, how long do you think that'll be?"

"Maybe thirty minutes. You don't have to wait if you don't want to. I can walk."

"No, I'll wait. Maybe we can get a bite to eat afterward."

"Ummm...sure, Dad," Lindsay says.

Emmitt hesitates. "Or maybe not. Maybe we'll just have leftovers."

"No," Lindsay says a bit too fast. "Let's go out. That'll be cool."

"Okay, I'm going to head over to the McDonald's while you finish up your test and come back to pick you up." Emmitt grins. "Good luck!"

After father and daughter say their goodbyes, Emmitt heads to the McDonald's across the street. Here the sun won't beam down on him, and he can enjoy a cold fountain drink in an air-conditioned fast-food restaurant.

* * *

With a few minutes to spare, Emmitt returns to Lindsay's school to wait for her. Emmitt patiently waits for Lindsay. He crunches on the ice cubes still slightly sweet from the second refill of soda. Though he could very easily take a few sips from the second cup he brought for Lindsay, he refrains because she would easily pick up on even the slightest hint that her cup has been tampered.

At five o'clock, Emmitt watches for Lindsay to exit the building. At a minute past, he calls her, but her phone goes to voicemail after several rings.

Maybe she's still finishing with the test, he thinks to himself.

He sends her a text. *I'm outside. Good luck on the test. Call me when you're coming out.*

Emmitt sets the phone down and stares intently at the door. It opens, and Lindsay's science teacher Mr. Bradley exits the building. The teacher walks toward the van.

"Hey, excuse me, Mr. Bradley!" Emmitt calls out. "Is my daughter Lindsay done with her test?"

"Yes, sir," replies Mr. Bradley. "She did a great job on the exam. B+."

Emmitt pauses. "Wow, so you've graded it already?"

Mr. Bradley nods and then raises his eyebrow. "Yeah, that was an hour ago. I graded her paper right after Lindsay left."

"Hey, Daddy," says Lindsay.

Emmitt and Mr. Bradley turn to see Lindsay standing next to the van. She grins and waves. Emmitt and Mr. Bradley exchange a glance.

"Lindsay, I thought you left," Mr. Bradley says.

"Oh, I did," blurts Lindsay. "I mean..." Lindsay pauses and giggles. "I mean, I went to the bathroom." She places a hand on her belly and grimaces. "I had a stomachache, but I'm better now."

"I tried calling and texting you," Emmitt says.

"Whoops," Lindsay says with another laugh as she pulls out her phone. "Sorry, bad reception in the building."

"Hey," Mr. Bradley lightly taps Emmitt on the arm with the back of his hand. "I've gotta run. Let me know if you need anything."

"Okay, thanks," Emmitt says while keeping his eyes

on Lindsay. She smiles and blinks slowly.

"Is it okay to get in the car now?" Lindsay asks as she reaches for the handle.

Emmitt nods, still watching her as she steps carefully, like she is just learning to walk. She is slightly off balance, though not in any danger of falling.

"Hey, girl," another girl, exiting the building, shouts with a wave. Her thin, dark-haired frame saunters over to Lindsay. "See ya tomorrow, huh?"

"Yeah, definitely," Lindsay says, giving this girl a big hug. When they release, Lindsay points to Emmitt. "Oh, sorry. Dad, this is Kay. She goes to afternoon school here as well."

"We'll see you around, Kay," Emmitt says flatly. "We need to go right now."

"Okay," Kay says with a pout. "Well, nice to meet you." Before leaving, she stretches out her arm and waves at Lindsay again. She skips off, and Emmitt watches her go in dumbfounded silence. He shakes his head suddenly as though clearing the strange encounter from his memory.

"You okay, Dad?" Lindsay asks with a slow and deliberate cheer in her voice. "Don't mind, Kay. She's good people."

"That's what I'm afraid of," Emmitt says. "Get in the van. You've got some explaining to do."

Lindsay complies and sits in the front passenger seat beside Emmitt. She brushes a lock of blonde hair away from her eyes and grins.

Emmitt looks into Lindsay's blue eyes. The sun's height in the late afternoon causes her eyes to glisten. It is difficult for him to tell whether she is high on something, but her behavior as she came up to the car as though nothing was wrong, indicates otherwise. He takes Lindsay's hand in his and continues to look into her eyes while he places his index finger on her wrist.

"You're acting kind of funny, Dad," Lindsay says. "Why are you looking at me like that?"

"Because you're high," Emmitt says sternly.

"Yeah." She looks away from Emmitt and leans back in the seat, and blinks slowly. "You're right. I'm high...just like you used to get."

"Shit, Lindsay!" Emmitt slams his hand on the steering wheel. "What'd she give you?"

Lindsay shrugs. "Oh, it was just..." She pauses and blinks twice. Then, she sighs and closes her eyes.

"Lindsay," Emmitt shakes her, but she doesn't respond. His heart beats rapidly in his chest. "Fuck!" He pounds the gas and races to the hospital. *Dear God, please hold onto my baby girl,* he thinks to himself.

One block, then another, and Emmitt does not stop or slow down for the patrol vehicle that follows with sirens blaring. Rather, he hits his four-way flashers and picks up speed. The officer behind him matches Emmitt's pace until they both pull up to the emergency drop off point at the hospital where a team is already waiting with a gurney to receive him.

"Sir, what's wrong?" a woman dressed in blue scrubs asks.

"She took something, a drug," stammers Emmitt. "I don't know what. One moment she was giggling and talkative, and the next moment she was passed out."

The woman listens and nods while the team she's with straps Lindsay to the gurney, checks her vitals, and hooks her up to an IV. She turns and follows the team in as they rush into the ER. Emmitt follows right behind, and the officer catches up to him and taps him on the shoulder.

"Sir," he says, "please hold for a moment."

"Are you giving me a ticket, or something?" Emmitt asks. "My daughter's not well."

"I'm sorry. I'm Deputy Crichton with the sheriff's department. No, I'm not giving you a ticket. I just need to write a preliminary report. I caught a bit of what you told the nurse. Please fill me in with a little more detail. What's your daughter's name and date of birth?"

"Lindsay Wasson. November 28, 1993."

"Do you know what she took?" Deputy Crichton asks.

Emmitt shakes his head. "No, but I do know who gave it to her, some girl named Kay. I've never seen her before."

"What does she look like?"

"Pale. Dark hair. She has that goth look about her."

Deputy Crichton writes down these details. "I'll be back with a follow-up. Take care. I wish your daughter a speedy recovery."

Emmitt thanks Deputy Crichton and stuffs his business card into his wallet.

Entering through the hospital sliding doors, Emmitt walks right up to the attendee's desk and hands over his insurance card.

"My daughter was just brought in," he says.

"Okay, what's her name and date of birth?" asks the attendee, a middle-aged woman. She taps at her keyboard. "It looks like she was just in a couple of months ago. Any changes in health or medication?"

"No, but she definitely took something this afternoon. She appeared high when I picked her up from school, and then she passed out."

The attendee nods and continues to type. "If you wait right in the seats over there, I'll let one of the nurses know that you're here."

"Can't I go see her?"

The attendee looks up and flashes him a weary smile. "I'm sorry. We need all the room we can, but I promise to get you when she's ready."

Emmitt takes a seat in the waiting room. He reflects on the strife and joy he has shared with Lindsay, and he hopes to make many more memories with her. He has been where Lindsay is now. Maggie, along with her father, were the ones to catch him when he finally hit rock bottom. Emmitt's only hope is that he can be as strong of an anchor for Lindsay as his wife was for him. Picking up the phone with the knowledge that he won't be able to do it alone, he dials his father-in-law's number.

The phone rings twice before Maggie's father Willis answers.

"Hello, Emmitt," says Willis. "It's been a long time. How's Lindsay?"

Swallowing hard, Emmitt can no longer hide from the truth. A few months ago, it seemed like just a fluke, but now he's not so certain.

"Pop, I think she's an addict," says Emmitt. He waits for Willis to respond, but the phone line goes quiet. "Willis, did you get that? Are you there?"

"I'm here, Emmitt," Willis says. "Claire and I can be there within a few hours if you need us."

"Please, I'd like that."

Though he never called on them while he and Lindsay were working through some of their past issues, Emmitt is thankful now for his courage to call and their willingness to help.

"Excuse me, Mr. Wasson," calls a female voice.

Emmitt looks up. The nurse who initially received Lindsay is standing just a few feet away. She holds a clipboard in her hand. When he makes eye contact with her, she smiles.

"Your daughter's waking up," the nurse continues. "Though she's a little groggy from her previous high, she's asking for you."

Standing, Emmitt nods and follows the nurse down a bright hallway and past a few dimly lit rooms until they stop in front of one closed door.

"Are you ready?" the nurse asks.

"I think so," Emmitt says. "Go ahead."

The nurse knocks on the door and opens it. They enter the room to the soft glow and sound of a beeping machine, monitoring Lindsay's vital signs.

"Daddy, is that you?" Lindsay asks. She ruffles her sheets in her hospital bed as she looks to Emmitt.

"I'm here, princess," Emmitt says. He takes a seat

beside her.

"I really fucked up, didn't I?" Lindsay says and chokes as she begins to cry. "You must hate me."

Although Emmitt prefers his daughter didn't curse in front of him, he lets it go. These past few months have been difficult for them both. Not to mention, he's let a few curse words slip from his mouth, too.

"No, don't say that," Emmitt says. "I love you. You could never do anything to make me hate you. I'll always be right here." Emmitt takes her hand, and this time she holds onto his.

Chapter Twenty

June 4, 2008

Emmitt awakes to a knock at the door. He sees that Lindsay is already up and has already finished breakfast. She appears to have been looking at him for quite some time, as if willing him to wake.

"Good morning," Emmitt says. "How'd you sleep?"

"All right, I guess," Lindsay says nonchalantly.

There is another knock at the door.

"You better get that," Lindsay says.

Emmitt opens the door to find Deputy Crichton there. His hat is off, and he wears a solemn expression.

"I'm sorry to disturb you, Mr. Wasson," says the deputy. "I heard your daughter is awake. I have a few questions for her."

"Sure, come in," says Emmitt. He leads the deputy into Lindsay's room and points to her bed. "Feel free to have a seat."

"Thank you, but I'll stand," replies the deputy. He turns to Lindsay. "Hello, young lady. I'm Deputy Crichton. Would you be able to answer some questions about Kay Mallon, the girl you were with yesterday?"

Lindsay looks nervously at Emmitt. When Emmitt gives her a reassuring glance, Lindsay turns back to the deputy and nods.

"Okay, thank you," says Deputy Crichton. "How long have you known her?"

"Not long, really," replies Lindsay. "We just met a few months ago. She only goes to afternoon school."

"Did she sell you any dope yesterday?"

Lindsay begins to fidget. "No, she just gave it to me free. She said it'll make me feel good, not like the last time I tried it."

"She overdosed on heroin back in April," blurts Emmitt. "It was a one-time deal."

"I see," says Deputy Crichton. He steps back and glances between Emmitt and Lindsay. "You'll probably want to get some professional help." He takes out three photographs, handing one to Emmitt and two to Lindsay. "These are pictures of Kay Mallon. We found her last night."

In the photograph, Emmitt sees the still form of Kay Mallon. Though he only just met her, he can see that her pale face bears the mark of death with wide staring eyes and gaping mouth.

"Oh, my God!" Lindsay cries. "She must've gone back for seconds or something. How did she..." Lindsay trails off and looks at the deputy.

"She was an addict," says Deputy Crichton. "Probably used for months or even years. Count yourself lucky. I came by because I thought you should know what could happen to you."

"Thank you, deputy," Emmitt says. He turns his attention to Lindsay as Deputy Crichton nods and makes his way out the door. With wet tears, Lindsay stares at her blankets. Emmitt sits beside her on the bed, and she shifts away from him, making enough room for him so that he doesn't fall off.

"Hey, Lindsay," he says as he looks into his daughter's watery blue eyes. "Let's get some help and put this behind us."

She nods and snuggles herself into his arms, and cries. In her tears, he can only hope that she has not trod too deeply down this path toward a nearly inescapable hell. Yet, no matter how far down she has gone, Emmitt will reach her, hold onto her, and pull her back himself.

CHAPTER TWENTY-ONE

January 7, 2009

It is a cold winter evening, and Emmitt is making another round of the warehouse and checking every door on his night guard duty. He heads to the front desk to log another uneventful hour. As a contractor, the company he works for has experienced a rise in petty theft, Emmitt has yet to discover a single person exiting the warehouse with anything stolen. So, not since the flood the previous year has Emmitt encountered anything other than a slightly ajar bathroom door.

He sits and documents his lack of finding while the previous shift guard prepares to leave for the night.

"Anything else you need before I go?" asks Larry, an elderly gentleman, enjoying his retirement as a part-time guard.

Emmitt glances up from his report. "No, I don't think so. Go on ahead."

As Larry opens the door and steps out into the chill of the night, Emmitt's personal phone rings. He grabs it from its holster and reads the caller ID showing Frank Burgess.

"Hold on a second while I take this," Emmitt says. Since discovering Lindsay's occasional drug use, Emmitt has been on higher alert. Though she hasn't had an episode with this recently, any call from Frank is a call that might warrant an emergency leave of absence from work.

He picks up the phone.

"Hey, Frank," says Emmitt. "Is Lindsay okay?" As Emmitt waits for Frank's reply, Larry waits with the door open, letting in a cold gust of air that chills Emmitt.

"No, I'm afraid not," Frank's voice comes over the phone. "We busted a woman with an attempt to sell. Lindsay was with her. We're not sure if she was selling or buying. She wouldn't say either, and we didn't press her. It's better to wait for you to be here. She's in a holding cell right now. We can hold her here for twenty-four hours, or you can pick her up now."

Emmitt glances at Larry still waiting by the door. The old man is clearly exhausted, yet this has very little effect on Emmitt's decision-making. In the past, Larry has covered dozens of times for other guards, often working double shifts simply because he had nothing better to do.

"You can hold her," Emmitt says. "Maybe a night in jail will sober her up and keep her from making any more mistakes."

"Alright, Emmitt. We'll keep her to a cell of her own, but the ruffians and vagabonds in here might influence her otherwise."

"I think they already did. Take care. I'll see you in the morning."

Emmitt hangs up, wondering if he indeed made the right decision.

"You need to go?" asks Larry. "I can stay."

"No, you go get your rest," Emmitt says. "I may still need you to cover for me later on in the week."

Alone at the guard station with only the buzzing of the lamps to keep him company, Emmitt sits. He passes the time by making double and sometimes triple rounds within each hour. This keeps his thoughts clear and his eyes more watchful, for simply sitting would cause him to delve deep into his soul, searching for some meaning behind Lindsay's apparent propensity to hang out with the wrong crowd. First, it was Troy, and then Kay. Now, she's with some random chick he's never met.

"What is Lindsay thinking?" Emmitt asks aloud on another round in the fourth hour of his shift, failing to avoid dwelling on his daughter's predicament. "I thought she was over this. Just two samples, and that's it."

It dawns on him now more than before that he has been in painfully obvious denial, especially as a person who has gone through this stage of drug use in the past. First, it starts as something casual. For Emmitt, it was the alcohol that drowned out the nightmares of combat overseas and losing many friends in the Gulf War. Later, when he had gone through treatment and thought he was free from addiction, the accident at work occurred. The accident propelled him into misusing very powerful opioids that would have killed him if not for his wife and his father-in-law, discovering him passed out in his bedroom.

Now, his daughter is addicted. She has barely scratched the surface, or at least that's what Emmitt is banking on. If he can keep her from going too deep, perhaps he can save her from destroying her life.

Emmitt leans back in his chair and sighs aloud. He's glad that at least Troy isn't in Lindsay's life anymore. The young man has another year in prison before he is released.

Grabbing letterhead template, Emmitt writes a leave request, hoping that two weeks would be enough time to keep his daughter out of a certain hell or pull her out. He wants to get her the treatment she desperately needs.

CHAPTER TWENTY-TWO

January 8, 2009

Sleep deprivation from a long night of worry while watchfully guarding the warehouse threatens to cause Emmitt to succumb to his own weariness of mind and body. The morning shift arrives. He stands up to get his blood flow circulating, so he can feel refreshed. The trick doesn't work. He can barely keep his eyes open when he finally exits the building and is shocked awake by a sudden gust of frosty air.

Though winter has yet to bring snow, it is unusually cold, and when Emmitt finally sits on the cold, hard surface of his aging van, he is fully awake. The internal temperature reads a dreadfully chilly negative five degrees, and with wind chill, the temperature outside is more like negative fifteen degrees.

Emmitt will have to forgo sleep for an indefinite amount of time. As he drives, the van warms up, yet not enough to match the core emotional temperature raging within him. Though he had all night to come to a resolution as to what he is going to do with Lindsay, he's still not sure, which troubles him. He thought devising a solution would be simple. He has been blessed with the ability to save her from her own destruction because he has been able to recognize, albeit rather late, her path of addiction.

Pulling up to the station, Emmitt wishes he had his wife here to guide him through what he anticipates will be a trying conversation.

Frank Burgess is the first and only person to greet Emmitt when he arrives. Emmitt suspects Frank has told his staff he would handle the situation. The two men sit in his office.

"I'm sorry, Emmitt," Frank says. "We're just not doing enough to protect her. To be honest, I am not sure you are doing enough to help her out."

Emmitt sits across from Frank in his office. Unaware that Emmitt has arrived to pick her up, Lindsay is still in her holding cell.

"We're still doing therapy," Emmitt says. "I've rearranged my schedule. I'm not sure what else I'm supposed to do. Do I need to follow her to school or wait for her in the parking lot?"

"No, that'll likely push her further in the wrong direction," says Frank. He rubs his chin thoughtfully. "Have you ever shared with her why you fell into your troubles with alcohol and then with the oxycodone?"

Emmitt shakes his head. "To be honest, Frank, I'm really not sure I can face that right now." He looks down at the floor, careful about what he is going to say to his oldest friend.

"You mean, you've never come to terms with it yourself?"

"I suppose I've just been avoiding the topic, even in therapy with Dr. Phillips."

"Well, if you don't come to terms, it'll bite you in the ass."

"Seems plain to me. Let's get Lindsay, so we can go home. I'm planning to take the next couple of weeks off."

"That's good." Frank picks up a receiver and requests

that Lindsay be released and brought down to his office. In a few minutes, Lindsay is at the door. She looks more exhausted than Emmitt feels. Her hair appears tangled, and lack of sleep has made her eyes bloodshot. In the doorway, she seems small, frightened, and defeated. Seeing her in this way, Emmitt stands and steps toward her, bridging the obvious expanse created between himself and his daughter due to her behavior and his apparent obliviousness to her need.

He wraps her in his arms and pulls her close while ignoring the smell of pot on her clothing. Though he embraces her to give her the warmth and comfort she so desperately needs, he might as well be wrapping himself around an inflexible mannequin. Lindsay feels rigid, and Emmitt fears he's already lost her.

Emmitt releases Lindsay and steps an arm's distance away from her while keeping his hand on her shoulders. He searches her eyes, but she looks away. She seems fixated on the floor as if she holds a silent communion with the speckled patterns on the tile.

"Lindsay, please look at me," Emmitt says in a firm, yet slightly soft tone.

When Lindsay does look into his eyes, he notices her eyes — red and swollen. Her cheeks bare the streaks of tears. She hasn't washed her face. He didn't get a call that she was absent from school, and he wonders where she has been since she left school and the time of her picked up last night.

"Where've you been?" he asks while being careful to keep his tone steady and concerned rather than accusatory.

Lindsay doesn't answer. She simply shrugs and walks down the hallway.

"We picked up her and the young lady she was with right on the outskirts of town," Frank chimes in. "It's where a lot of drug activity has been occurring."

"Who was she with?" asks Emmitt.

"We can't say. No one you would know, but a woman

much too old to be hanging out with a sixteen-year-old."

"Shit," Emmitt says. "Might as well take her home and get her cleaned up unless she's being charged with something."

"Nothing. The officers who picked them up couldn't tell whether she was buying or selling. Hopefully, this short time in jail will wake her up. God knows that seeing her friend dead didn't."

From the hallway, Lindsay lets out a muffled cry. When Emmitt peaks into the hallway, he sees her, squatting against the wall, with the end of her sleeve in her mouth. She chews on her sleeve to mask the sound of her sobs.

"Lindsay, it's time to go," Emmitt says quietly. He waits for her to stand, but she remains where she is. Emmitt kneels, puts both arms beneath her, and lifts her like he used to do when she was younger. Holding her in his arms, with her head to his right and her feet dangling to his left, he is surprised at how light she has gotten. She used to be a ferocious eater, especially during the soccer season. Now she seemed underweight compared to her healthy athletic build in the past.

"Let's get you home," Emmitt says quietly. "It seems we've been away for far too long."

CHAPTER TWENTY-THREE

January 9, 2009

Awakened in the night by a slight shift in his bed, Emmitt rolls over to find Lindsay nestled next to him, where his wife used to sleep. He faces her. Lindsay's breathing is steady, and her face appears to glow under the illumination of the moonlight. The worry lines have all but vanished on her face, and she seems to almost smile in her sleep. Emmitt caresses her face gently, thinking back to many times when Lindsay would join him and Maggie in bed when she couldn't sleep. There is very little difference between his daughter now, and when she was young, only her restlessness is due to a very real nightmare threatening to drag her to her own living hell.

Lindsay opens her eyes. The corners of her lips curve until the dimples in her cheeks appear. Emmitt moves his hand away.

"Sorry," he says. "I didn't mean to wake you."

"It's okay, Daddy," says Lindsay. "I didn't mean to wake you up either. I just couldn't sleep." Lindsay shakes her head and sits up, pulling the comforter close to her.

"We've really got to get you some help, you know. I've made an appointment for you to see Dr. Phillips tomorrow morning."

"I don't want to see her right now." Lindsay whines.

"Why not?"

"Because..." she trails off, grasping as she used to do for some excuse that would wiggle her out of doing something she didn't want to do. "I just don't want to. Besides, I have school tomorrow."

"School can wait, Lindsay. This can't. We need to get you some help."

"I know." She lays back down, face up on the pillow but doesn't close her eyes. She is thinking, processing, and Emmitt would give just about anything to find out what is going through her head.

"You can sleep here for the rest of the night," Emmitt says. "If you want to talk, I'm here. Just wake me up."

Emmitt lays down. He rolls over so that his back is to Lindsay. Even he doesn't close his eyes, preferring to wait her out instead.

The night drags on for Emmitt as he listens to Lindsay, snoring quietly and creating for him the ambient sound he needs to lull him to sleep.

Awakening in the morning, Emmitt finds that Lindsay is already up.

"Lindsay," he calls out. When she doesn't answer, he calls out her name even louder.

"Here, I am," Lindsay says as she steps into the bedroom. Unlike last night, her hair looks clean and neatly brushed. She wears a pale, yellow sweater, faded blue jeans, and a ponytail. Her bright apparel makes her glow, and Emmitt smiles.

"Why are you looking at me like that?" Lindsay asks.

"You look very pretty today, princess, a lot like your mother," Emmitt says.

"Uh...thanks, I guess." Lindsay smiles back and does a curtsy. "I figured since we're seeing Dr. Phillips, I should try to look presentable."

If Emmitt hadn't known the mess she was in, he would have taken her for a calm and confident teen peppered with just enough spunk to give her parents a hard time, but not so much to give her parents heartache and grief.

"What's with the change of heart?" Emmitt asks.

Lindsay shrugs. "It's gonna happen either way, so why not today?"

"That's a good attitude, princess. Why don't you fix us a quick bite for breakfast before we go? I'll be down in a few minutes."

With the room to himself, Emmitt cannot help but voice a prayer for thanks that his daughter is ready to come around. She seems ready to get herself on the right track before she slips away from him.

In fifteen minutes, Emmitt is cleaned and dressed and comes downstairs. He is greeted by two plates of scrambled eggs still steaming with a side of toast on the kitchen table. He wants to eat breakfast with Lindsay, but she is nowhere around.

Before Emmitt can panic, the front door creaks open. Lindsay stands at the entrance with a rolled-up newspaper. Her mouth gapes open, but she quickly closes it.

"Oh," she hesitates. "You're ready. Let's eat."

An engine outside roars, and Emmitt pivots his stance just in time to see a faded red sedan race down the street. He shuts the door and glares at Lindsay. They stay still for a moment, staring at each other, until Lindsay breaks eye contact and looks to the floor.

"Who was that?" asks Emmitt.

"No one," says Lindsay nervously. "He's just the paperboy."

"The paperboy doesn't drive a red sedan. I'll take the paper, though."

Biting her lower lip, Lindsay hands Emmitt the newspaper, which he opens slowly. As he unravels it, he glances at Lindsay to read her expression, but she avoids eye contact. Once Emmitt has fully opened it, he realizes why Lindsay won't look at him. Emmitt's stomach drops when the contents of the newspaper reveal a little baggie of fine powder. Lindsay could have easily stuffed this in her pocket in the time it took her to turn away from the door when he came down, but she didn't.

"Well," Emmitt says, "looks like that guy was delivering something."

"Please don't be mad," Lindsay pleads.

"I'm not mad,. I'm fed up."

Before Lindsay can even react, Emmitt strides to the sink, turns on the faucet and garbage disposal, and then dumps the powder into the sink. Lindsay screeches but doesn't make a move to stop him.

"I don't think I even want to know how you were able to buy any of this," Emmitt says when he finally turns off the water and the garbage disposal. "Let's eat."

Emmitt sits at the table and looks with expectation at Lindsay to sit down. He can tell by the way she fidgets in place with her clothing and hair that she is experiencing a withdrawal. He realizes the ticks were there all along, masked by her over enthusiasm to go see Dr. Phillips. When she doesn't move to sit, he shovels another forkful of eggs into his mouth and chews.

"These are very good," he says between bites of food. He takes a moment to finish his bite. "Are you really not hungry?"

Lindsay shakes her head. Her watery blue eyes stare back at him from where she stands at the front door. Not even an hour ago, her eyes and her pouty lips donned the façade of a well-adjusted teen. How could Emmitt have missed this? He sighs and puts down his fork.

"You know, I've been where you are now," he says. "I know the way out. You just have to trust me." Emmitt goes to the counter and fixes two cups of black coffee. "This'll help take the edge off, but I need you to sit down first."

Lindsay sits down and imitates Emmitt. She sips her

coffee and eats her food, savoring each bite as if it's her last.

"We're not going to Dr. Phillips," Emmitt says. "Not directly anyway."

Holding the steaming mug in both of her hands, Lindsay sips her coffee in obedience, as if she's come to an understanding that her fate at the moment is in Emmitt's hands.

"Let's finish eating," continues Emmitt. "It looks like you're going to be away from home for a little while, okay?"

"But I want to stay here," Lindsay whimpers.

"I'm sorry, you can't, but I'll be with you every step of the way."

Chapter Twenty-Four

March 10, 2009

Like waking up from a recurring nightmare, Emmitt breathes deeply, trying to slow down his heart rate. He sits outside the same drug rehabilitation program he resided in years ago. He wonders if this is how Maggie felt moments before walking inside to finally taking him home. Filled with joy and fear, Emmitt steps out of the van and heads inside.

At the time, his wife overwhelmed him with such an outpouring of love that he simply let it all wash over him, barely returning her love in kind. Now, he realizes he should have acted differently. Unless one leaves rehab with the conscious resolution to go forth and "sin no more," one will fall back into the old routine once surrounded by the familiar.

Though Emmitt didn't fall back into his old routines, his mistake was his simple existence. Life passed him by for so many years until his wife died. This, he decides upon finding his daughter's room, is something that he cannot let happen to Lindsay. She must be an active participant in life, not an empty vessel that could jeopardize the work she has accomplished in the past few months.

"Dad!" Lindsay exclaims as she stands. Her eyes, once wide with the wonder of innocence, are now clouded with the experience that comes through enduring adversity.

Emmitt embraces his daughter.

"Are you ready to go, princess?" he asks. Lindsay nods eagerly, and Emmitt notices Father Klein, sitting in a chair in the corner of the room. Father Klein stands and extends his hand.

"Good to see you again, Emmitt," Father Klein says.

Though over the past few months, Emmitt has had the occasion to talk to his pastor, the circumstances here are obviously different. Emmitt supposes Father Klein had been counseling Lindsay about her addiction.

"Your daughter and I have just been talking," continues Father Klein. "She is resolute in her decision to abstain from the drug use, but she is also resolute in her decision to get all of you, including the Burgesses' back to church. It's been too long."

Emmitt looks at Lindsay. She gives him a slight smile.

"I just went to confession, too," she chirps. "We need to go back to church."

Words evade Emmitt as he seeks a response. True, it has been years since he has been to church, but why is Father Klein now suddenly inviting them? Where was he a year after his wife's death, the string of robberies, and Troy's relationship with Lindsay? Then again, Emmitt hasn't even felt God's presence during the past few life events. He's been doing all of this by himself for so long.

With expectation in their eyes, Lindsay and Father Klein gaze at Emmitt.

"Sure," he finally says. "Yeah, we can go back to church."

"That's great to hear, Emmitt!" cheers Father Klein. "If you're interested, we can also have confession right now. Or you can come by Saturday afternoon."

Emmitt chuckles. "I see you haven't lost your old touch." Thinking back, Emmitt remembers the old priest has always been direct, so offering confession on the spot is nothing unusual for him. Emmitt smiles and extends his hand to Father Klein.

"I'll see you at church, Father," he says.

Wishing them well, Father Klein leaves Emmitt and Lindsay alone to ponder their thoughts, their fears, and their hopes for a brighter future.

"Well, kiddo, you ready?" asks Emmitt.

"Yep," Lindsay says, throwing a small duffle bag over her shoulders, leading the way out of the room and down the hall.

Emmitt follows with an anxious heart. First, he cannot begin to imagine what it will be like to support Lindsay throughout the rest of her recovery—knowing full well that exiting the rehabilitation program is only the first step. The second and even longer step is remaining drug free. He knows as much from his own experience. Also, counseling with Dr. Phillips and Lindsay's own rehab counselor confirmed for him that the second step is long. Second, he cannot begin to imagine exactly what it will be like to return to church and to begin his return by going to confession. He can't even remember how long it's been since he's gone to church.

Awkward silence plays like a waltzing dirge between Emmitt and Lindsay as they ride home.

Although Lindsay insists on driving to get her the much-needed practice before taking her driving test, Emmitt refuses. He believes she needs to demonstrate more responsibility, to which Lindsay reluctantly agrees with him.

"You know we've got a lot of time to make up at school," says Emmitt.

"Yeah, I don't want to talk about it," Lindsay says. "I did a lot of the work already."

"Okay, are you thinking about starting up soccer

again? It'll be good for you."

"Maybe." Lindsay grows silent, casting her gaze out the window as Emmitt drives on.

He takes the not-so-subtle hint from his daughter that she doesn't want to talk. He understands that she probably wants to take a break from talking because she and Emmitt would talk during her therapy sessions. He used to visit her daily until Lindsay had explained she needed to do the work on her own. Emmitt let her have her space, limiting himself to a few visits a week. He had hoped she would ask him to come back more, but she never did. Glancing at Lindsay, Emmitt sighs and places his right arm around her shoulder.

"I'm glad to have you back," he says.

"I'm glad to be back," Lindsay says flatly. Emmitt hopes that her attitude will change when they pull up to the house because he has a surprise for her.

The rest of the ride passes in silence except for the sounds of the road. Emmitt veers the van onto their street. Ahead their house features many colorful decorations.

"Really, Dad?" asks Lindsay. Her tone is dripping with sarcasm, but Emmitt ignores it.

"What's the matter?" he asks. "It's just a little welcome home party." Emmitt grins and pulls into the driveway. He sees that confetti and twice as many balloons were added to the decorations after he left to pick up Lindsay.

"It looks like our friends were busy getting you ready for your arrival," says Emmitt.

"I didn't really want a party," Lindsay whispers as though afraid that those within the house would hear her protest.

"Hey, princess, look at me. You are loved by so many people. They've been praying for your return. They'll be glad to see you."

"Please, Dad, don't make me go." Lindsay frowns.

Though sixteen, Lindsay's pleading reminds Emmitt that she is still a kid.

"I'm sorry, Lindsay," Emmitt says. "If I had known I—
"

"How could you? You didn't ask."

Lindsay's combativeness surprises Emmitt. "What's wrong?" He realizes the work he needs to do with Lindsay starts now.

"Nothing," Lindsay says. Then, suddenly her attitude changes. "Actually, let's go in. I think I'm ready." She flashes Emmitt a grin that sparkles, even in her eyes. With a click, she pops her door open and hops out.

Emmitt gets out more slowly, distrusting the change he just witnessed. "Hey, I'll get your bag."

"Oh, wait!" Lindsay quickly meets Emmitt at the trunk.

"What's wrong?" Emmitt pops the trunk and reaches for her bag, which Lindsay snatches as soon as he catches hold of one of the handles. Her action causes an object to career out of the bag and fly through the space between Emmitt and Lindsay, whose wide eyes reveal shock and horror just as the object lands on the ground with a rattle and rolls to stop.

"What's this?" Emmitt asks, stepping toward the object.

"It's nothing!" Lindsay shouts. Her pitch has heightened to the point that it seems unrecognizable to Emmitt. He can't believe it's his daughter's voice.

From the pavement, Emmitt picks up what seemed like a recently used syringe. He holds it up.

"What is this?" he asks expectantly.

"It's mine," Lindsay says sadly.

"You don't appear to be high. When did you last use this?"

Lindsay shrugs. "Maybe a couple weeks ago."

"How did you pass the drug test?" Emmitt asks.

Lindsay does not give an answer, and there is no need for an answer. Emmitt knows full well that she must have received a urine sample from someone else. He ponders how she pulls off the strategy.

Emmitt looks at Lindsay, and he can only find within his heart disappointment and hurt. She looks at him with eyes conveying the guilt of one caught in the act of hiding a dirty little secret. They stand like that, not at all needing the words that silence itself conveys, while friends and family wait in bated anticipation for one recovered soul who will not arrive as scheduled.

Behind them, the front door opens. Daniella Burgess, who planned Lindsay's homecoming, peaks by the door. "Is everything all right?" she asks.

Emmitt and Lindsay remain engaged in a standstill of wills, neither giving way to the other while they both ignore Daniella, who descends the porch steps and comes between them.

"Hey, what's going on?" Daniella asks as she looks from Emmitt to Lindsay.

"Tell her, Lindsay," Emmitt says without taking his eyes off her. "If you don't tell her, I will."

"Tell me what?" Daniella asks. She steps closer to Lindsay and touches her shoulder, which makes Lindsay flinch.

"I found a needle with her things," Emmitt says.

"But it wasn't mine," Lindsay retorts. Then, she shakes her head. "I mean. It's mine, but I didn't use it."

"So, are you finished?" Daniella asks. "You're no longer using?"

"Not since I started the program."

"Then, why do you have this needle?" Emmitt asks.

"I took it from someone in the program."

"Lindsay, that doesn't make sense."

"She brought it in, and I didn't want her using, so I kept it."

"Why?" Daniella asks.

"I don't know," Lindsay replies. "Will it help if I say I'm sorry?"

"Sorry isn't really going to work here, Lindsay," Emmitt says. "You better be glad that all these people are waiting for you because I would just as well take you back."

"No, you wouldn't," Lindsay mumbles under her breath.

Emmitt exchanges a glance with Daniella who takes a cue from him.

"Hey, Lindsay," Daniella says. When Lindsay doesn't look up, Daniella steps toward her and takes her chin in her hand like she is a little child. Surprisingly, Lindsay doesn't pull away.

"Lindsay," Daniella repeats. "We're working really hard here to help you out. You have to meet us halfway."

"I know," Lindsay says, even quieter than before. "Why don't you all just drug test me, or something. That's what they did inside."

"Oh, we will," Emmitt says. "That was already a plan. Daniella, why don't you take her inside, and I'll dispose of this needle."

Daniella nods and leads Lindsay upstairs. As they head up, Lindsay stops and faces Emmitt.

"Hey, Dad, are you going to take Father Klein up on his offer?" she asks.

"What do you mean?" he asks.

"I mean, are you going to go to confession and church? I think that'll be good for you. Us. Me."

Emmitt hesitates. "Sure, we'll try to get there."

Daniella gives Emmitt a nod while she takes Lindsay inside. Though this encourages Emmitt, he is still reluctant to commit to anything specific. Not until he begins to see a change in his daughter. If that happens, then maybe he will show up.

Left to himself, Emmitt drops the syringe on the ground and stomps on it. With his heel, he grinds it into the pavement as though doing so will eradicate the addiction still within his daughter. Beneath his heel, the plastic tubing cracks into tiny pieces until the stainless-steel tip is all that remains. To dispose of the tip, he plucks a leaf from a nearby tree, using it as a buffer, to wrap the remainder of the needle in it. He throws this away, burying it between two bags of trash picked up the following morning.

With this operation complete, Emmitt ascends the porch steps and stops. Turning around, he sits and looks out upon the quiet of the neighborhood. Never one for parties, not even his own, he just needs a moment.

Yes, the counseling he received from Father Klein was helpful. Though Emmitt is not an atheist by any means, he also wouldn't attribute any of the priest's advice to him as coming directly from God, either. So, if God wants to really impress Emmitt, he is going to have to show up in a big way. Maybe free Lindsay completely of this addiction. And, oh, by the way, take care of Troy as well. That'll do it, too. He hasn't been around for a while, but he is sure to come again. When he does, Emmitt doesn't want him influencing Lindsay again. He looks up to the sky.

"God," he declares, "maybe you can do something about that piece of shit Troy." Emmitt balls his fist. "He's done enough damage in Lindsay's life. Can you keep him away? Because if you can't, I will."

Emmitt opens the front door, and a scene of warm, welcoming embraces unfolds before him. In the center of it all, stands Lindsay. She has managed to mask her deceit with a smile that radiates light out of her eyes onto each person she greets.

Chapter Twenty-Five

September 10, 2009

Six months pass with relatively mundane activity as Emmitt and Lindsay work to repair the damage to their relationship. Emmitt decides it wouldn't hurt to take Lindsay to church. When they go to church, Emmitt has decided he'll sit with her. Not only this, but Lindsay proves her resolve to remain drug free. Each random drug test comes back negative, and the only reason, Emmitt concludes, is Lindsay's renewed faith. Still, Emmitt has his doubts, so he continues the drug testing.

Six months or so clean, and one test comes back positive, showing that Lindsay has been smoking pot.

"Who's your supplier?" Emmitt asks in demanding tone.

"For what, Dad?" Lindsay asks. "I'm not taking heroin. You know that."

"Yeah, but pot. Really, Lindsay?"

"It's just pot, Dad. It's no big deal."

"You're not stupid, Lindsay. First pot, then something else. That's the way these things work for addicts. Believe me, I know."

"Is that the way it was for you?"

Emmitt purses his lips. "No, but addiction starts small. That's what I mean."

"But it's just —"

"It's not just anything. Where are you getting it from?"

"Please, Dad. Don't —"

"Is it Troy? I know he's out of jail. You need to stay away from him."

Lindsay doesn't respond, not for a long time. Rather she stares coldly at Emmitt.

"Fine, let's call, and we'll see what Leo has to say," says Emmitt.

"No, don't call!" Lindsay shouts as she rushes to Emmitt and swipes his phone from his hand. "I'll tell you, but I want you to promise you won't be mad."

Emmitt sits. "Lindsay, I can't promise that. If you're doing something that's going to ruin your life, I'm..."

He looks at Lindsay, with her bright blue eyes locking with his own dark eyes. He waits for her to speak. Several times her mouth opens, but no words come out. She breathes in as if searching for the right words to say.

"I just... can't... not... here..." Lindsay stammers at last and turns away from Emmitt. When she makes to walk up the steps, Emmitt rushes toward her and gently places his hands on her shoulders so that if she wanted to, she could still walk away. When she doesn't, Emmitt gently turns her around and pulls her into an embrace.

"I'm here, Lindsay. We're gonna get over this together or not at all. You hear me?" Emmitt steps away, so that he and Lindsay are only an arm's length from each other. "Shall we do this with Dr. Phillips? Maybe she can fit us in tomorrow?"

She nods. "Yeah, I think tomorrow will be okay."

"Great." Emmitt holds out his hand, to which Lindsay slaps him a high-five. When his palm remains open, Lindsay gives him a confused expression.

"Dad, why is your hand still out?" she asks.

"I need my phone, princess, to dial the therapist," he

replies.

"Oh, yeah." Lindsay giggles, and the tension within the room seems to melt away. She pulls out his phone from her back pocket and hands it to him. Emmitt calls Dr. Phillips' office. The line doesn't ring long before the receptionist answers.

"Dr. Phillips' office," chirps the receptionist. "How may I help you?"

"Hello," Emmitt says. "My daughter Lindsay and I would like to set up a therapy session at your earliest time."

"One moment please." In the background, the receptionist taps and clicks at her keyboard. "We have an opening today, but you would have to arrive in thirty minutes. Would that work for you?"

Emmitt freezes. He knows he can make it to the doctor's office in time, but he feels uneasy about going. If he and Lindsay go to this appointment, they will have to discuss their feelings. Emmitt pulls the phone away from his ear and looks to Lindsay for an answer.

"Do you think we can make it to the appointment today, princess?" he asks. Emmitt waits for Lindsay's response with bated breath.

"Yeah, we can do that," Lindsay says. She gives Emmitt two thumbs up, and then he confirms the appointment for today.

"Okay, let's go," he says.

Emmitt and Lindsay head in the car for the appointment.

* * *

The wait is an endless staring contest between Emmitt and the door as he sits outside of Dr. Phillip's office while Lindsay convenes with the doctor. Lindsay wanted to talk things out with her first. Something akin to waiting outside of a confessional, the muffled voices of Lindsay and the doctor only serve to heighten his nerves as he listens to the ambient sounds of the waiting room — the flipping of a magazine, the sliding of the secretary's glass door, and the fidgeting of a child with a wooden play set. In his waiting, Emmitt blocks these sounds out, choosing only to focus on the door before him and the impending conversation, looming just behind the door.

"Emmitt Wasson," the secretary calls.

Emmitt jumps to his feet, knocking the chair back into the wall.

"Sorry," he says and checks the wall. "I don't think I damaged anything."

"It's okay," says the secretary. "Go ahead in. They're ready for you."

He nods and opens the door until he sees Lindsay in her usual seat, facing Dr. Phillips. The doctor flashes him an inviting smile, but it does little to calm Emmitt's nerves. Lindsay won't look at him, even though she sits next to him.

"It's okay, Lindsay," Dr. Phillips says. "Just tell him everything you told me."

Emmitt has resolved to neither coax his daughter nor interrupt her for a response. A false move in either direction would most assuredly cause Emmitt to lose Lindsay. If he loses Lindsay, then he believes he would be no different than Leo, who lost Troy.

"Dad, I'm sorry," Lindsay says finally. "With you at work all the time, I just needed..." Lindsay stops.

Emmitt's heart thuds rapidly in his chest as he breathes in, trying to make sense of Lindsay's vague confession, or at least that's what he thinks it is.

"Troy didn't give me the pot," Lindsay continues. "He's not even allowed on school property. He's too old, I think. That's what he told me anyway." Lindsay pauses and looks at Emmitt. Although Emmitt wants to interrupt, he remains quiet. He's more interested in finding out how Lindsay found time to meet Troy and talk to him. When the silence becomes almost unbearable for Emmitt, he clears his throat.

"Go ahead, kiddo," he whispers. "I'm listening."

Lindsay gives a weak smile. "I got the pot from a girl at school. I just needed a little something since I haven't had... well, you know." Lindsay looks shamefully to Emmitt before she continues. "Troy told me not to take it, but I..."

Emmitt scoffs. He doesn't mean to make a sound, but he can't help himself. The idea of Troy, being helpful, seems unlikely.

"I'm serious, Dad," whines Lindsay. "You'd like Troy now that he's changed. He's different, in a good way, since prison. I think. And well..." Lindsay pauses and bites her lip. "I love him."

Emmitt leans forward in his chair, gulping back a torrent of emotion and half-digested bits of breakfast that. He stands and takes two giant steps to the water cooler behind him. Steadying himself with one hand on the cooler, he snatches a cone paper cup and pushes the water lever down, filling the cup to the brim. Then, he guzzles it down. On his second cup, he turns and sips more slowly, taking in his daughter's gaze until she breaks and looks to Dr. Phillips. The doctor gently places her hand on Lindsay's shoulder. At this, Emmitt crumples and tosses the cup into the trash can as he passes his seat across from his daughter and sits directly next to her on the couch.

Pulling her close with one arm, he kisses Lindsay on her temple, and relaxes his embrace until she looks with raised eyebrows at him.

"Dad, please don't be mad at me," she says.

"I'm not," he says softly. "I know you love him, Lindsay. It took me a long time to admit this to myself." Emmitt sucks his teeth. "I don't think he's good for you, not right now. Can you wait until you're done with high school, at least?"

Lindsay nods. "I thought you'd say that, and so did Dr. Phillips. I just... I just needed to tell you."

"Is there anything else?" Emmitt searches her eyes.

Lindsay shakes her head. "Thank you, daddy. You know, for listening."

"Well, I think that's enough for one day," says Dr. Phillips as she stands. "Remember, Emmitt, we still have a lot of work to do together. This, I think, is going to take you and your daughter a long way."

On that day, Dr. Phillips is right. For the next year, from September 2009 to September 2010, Lindsay's life is all about studying hard, going to school, playing soccer, and coming home. During this time, Emmitt even agrees to see Troy a few times. Emmitt admits Troy appears to have truly changed. Still, he forbids the young man to be alone with his daughter. Troy is out of high school, while Lindsay is only sixteen years old. Lindsay, by all appearances, happily abides.

Chapter Twenty-Six

April 12, 2011

A façade, no matter how mundane it may appear, is only that, which is an idea that Emmitt carries with him throughout the year and half since this breakthrough with Dr. Phillips' guidance. Until that is, the pretense is pricked, and the guise crumbles under the weight of reality. Though she hides it well, Lindsay is still an addict. Emmitt sees this in her grades, in the company she keeps, and the way she abandons her love for the game of soccer.

Her actions peak when Emmitt waits with mounting certainty that his daughter will not come home. He notices the signs. Earlier in the day, she texts him, saying that she has to make up some work after school. Though her track record has been riddled with questionable activity after school, he approves because, as Lindsay points out, she has come home on time every day for the last thirty days. They make an agreement, and he allows her to stay late. He figures he does not want to hinder her academic progress with only a few months away from graduation.

Now an hour later, after Emmitt lets Lindsay stay out, he realizes his mistake. He stares at his phone. The messaging app is open. The little bars beneath his most recent message indicate his message has been read, but not replied to. He switches to his contacts and scrolls through until he comes upon Frank Burgess's name. He calls.

"Hey, Emmitt," Franks says over the phone. "I'm in the middle of—"

"This'll be quick, though," Emmitt interrupts. "Lindsay hasn't come home. Can you put a trace on her phone and find out where she is?"

"Shit do you think—"

"I do. But I hope she just got caught up at school."

"I'll tell you what? I'll have one of our deputies follow up with you when they find out where she is."

With a quick thanks, Emmitt ends the call and proceeds to berate his lack of foresight. Somehow between her lack of freedom to go wherever she pleases and her sudden opportunity to demonstrate her trustworthiness, Lindsay has managed to get away from him. If found, he hopes to find her well and drug free. *Once an addict, always an addict.* He ponders this phrase, hoping it isn't true, not for his daughter. And even after being clean and sober for years, Emmitt knows that addiction can still creep up on someone.

Emmitt decides to make one more call as a courtesy to Leo Andreadis.

"Emmitt, my friend, it's been too long," says Leo when he answers the call. "What can I do for you?"

"Do you know where your son is?" Emmitt asks.

"Yeah, he's here with me. Why?"

"Put him on. I want to talk to him."

Leo pauses on the line. "Sorry, I can't find him."

Emmitt huffs. "But you just told me he was with you."

"He was." There is hesitation in Leo's voice, like he is choosing his next words carefully. "I mean, maybe an hour ago, he was here, playing cards and drinking beers."

Then, he went up to his room."

"Have you seen Lindsay?"

"No," Leo says almost too quickly. "She would be in school anyway, wouldn't she?"

"Right now?" Emmitt asks. "No, it's well past five o'clock. She should be home right now."

"Oh, well I haven't seen her, not today anyway. She was around yesterday."

Emmitt doesn't reply. Like yesterday, he usually meets Lindsay after school lets out, and he'll drive her home. Emmitt concludes that Lindsay may not have gone to school yesterday, or she left after her teachers noted her attendance. Emmitt wonders how long Lindsay has been deceiving him.

"You alright, Emmitt?" Leo asks.

"No, I'm not okay," Emmitt says. "Tell your son when you see him to stay away from Lindsay!"

"Or what?" Leo scoffs. "Are you going to throw him down some stairs again?"

"Let's just say you don't want to find out."

Without a goodbye, Emmitt hangs up the phone.

"Fuck!" Emmitt shouts and runs upstairs.

From his pocket, he pulls out a key ring and thumbs through it until he finds a small key that he inserts into the lock of a drawer by his bedside. Pulling the drawer out reveals a nine-millimeter handgun, a simple thing he's kept in the house for years without even thinking about it. Opening another drawer reveals two magazines, one of which he inserts into the gun, then he stuffs the gun in his jeans right at the small of his back where it would stay hidden and available should he need it later.

Without another thought, he darts downstairs. Before he reaches the door, another call comes in. This is from the sheriff's department.

"Mr. Wasson, this is Deputy Jeffreys," says the deputy.

"Tell me you found Lindsay," he pleads.

"No, but we traced her. She's on Washington Ave and Main Street. You know the place?"

"Yeah, I do."

Emmitt knows the place is dangerous, especially for Lindsay. Although she's getting older, he still views her as his little girl. The idea of Lindsay out on her own terrifies Emmitt. Her being out with Troy would make matters worse.

"Me and my partner will go out there together and get her," continues Jeffreys. "You sit tight, okay?"

"Sure, I can do that," lies Emmitt. "I appreciate it."

"That's great, sir. We'll bring your daughter home when we track her down."

"Thanks. Good luck."

And lock up that fucker Troy while you're at it, Emmitt thinks to himself. He wishes he could say that over the phone as he ends the call with the deputy. Stepping out of the house and locking the door behind him, Emmitt gets in the van, puts the keys in the ignition, and heads on the road with every intention of arriving at the "scene of the crime," at least ten minutes before the cops arrive. He plans to have the element of surprise when he pulls into that neighborhood, especially since he will be armed. Troy won't be expecting him.

As expected, Emmitt appears to be the first one on scene. The streets of Washington and Main are littered with trash, and several of the houses are boarded up. If not for the deputy's call, Emmitt would think this place is uninhabitable. Some activity to Emmitt's right draws his attention to a corner store. The flashing sign on its window reads "lottery sold here," and its door jingles open.

Emmitt parks and walks toward the corner store. He is aware of the cool bulge of metal, pressing against the small of his back and moving with a swagger that matches his own as he approaches five young men, blocking the doorway. Just as he passes through them, one of the guys steps into his pathway.

"I'm not looking for trouble," Emmitt says. "Just looking for my daughter and her boyfriend." Emmitt hands the youth a photo of Lindsay. "This is my daughter. She's five-foot three."

The youth hands Emmitt the photo. "We haven't seen her," says the youth as he hands the picture back to Emmitt. "Who's her boyfriend?'

"Troy."

The youth grins. "We know Troy, but he hasn't been around for a while. Not since the police picked him up."

"Thanks, anyway." Emmitt extends a hand.

The youth shakes Emmitt's hand. "No problem. The name's Marco. If you're daughter's here, it's probably not for anything good."

Emmitt nods. "Thanks for the tip, Marco. You mind if I call around here again?"

"We'll be here. Just don't come after dark. It gets hot around here."

Emmitt heads back to his van. Though he was expecting to be finished and out of here before the cops arrived, the neighborhood is almost too quiet. News, Emmitt assumes, will travel fast in this neighborhood, and the presence of police activity would certainly be news. Unless, of course, he is wrong, or he got here much sooner than police could have.

Once in the van, Emmitt checks his mirrors. The youths are still hanging out by the corner store as though his presence has only mildly annoyed them. Marco gives Emmitt a final wave, and Emmitt returns the gesture before leaving the parking lot. Once on the street, Emmitt hits the gas and races down Washington toward home. He keeps an eye out for police cruisers that would certainly be a part of the oncoming traffic.

About a mile out, Emmitt's phone rings.

"Hello," he says.

"Emmitt, where are you?" Frank asks.

"I stepped out."

"Yeah, I can see that. I'm out in front of your house.

I've got some bad news. You want it now or when you get home?"

"Now's fine."

"We found Lindsay's phone in a dumpster. We're currently doing a search for her in the neighborhood."

"What neighborhood was that, Frank?"

"The one we told you. Washington and Main."

"Bullshit, Frank. I was just there."

Frank pauses. "Shit, Emmitt. I'm sorry. We didn't want you to get in the way."

"Whatever, you gave me the wrong information. Mind telling me where her phone was?"

"Main and New Hampshire. A few miles down the road from Washington. It's much worse there. It wouldn't be safe for you."

"Thanks," Emmitt says. He tosses the phone down and squeals his wheels into a dangerously tight U-turn. The turn threatens to roll the van, but it hugs the turn well enough to straighten out and speed down Main Street. He flies down past the corner store where the youth still mill about. In the corner of his eye, he notices one of them point as he races by, and he sees through his rearview mirror that the kids watch him until he is out of sight.

In a few minutes, Emmitt slows the van and parks it right behind a line of patrol vehicles and gets out. An officer approaches.

"Mr. Wasson, I presume," says the officer as he extends his hand to Emmitt. "I'm Detective Kennedy. Sheriff Burgess phoned ahead and said you were on your way."

"I'm sure he did," Emmitt says sarcastically.

The detective nods. "I'm sorry. There's really nothing more you can do here. We're currently knocking on all doors. It's best you head home. You're likely to be in the way if you don't."

Emmitt groans. "It's okay. I'll stay. I won't be in the way."

159

"But if you interfere—"

"I won't."

"Well, suit yourself then," Detective Kennedy shrugs and walks off. He begins to shout out orders to a couple of officers standing around. They give him a nod and make their way to another door, and knock.

As the sun sets upon the neighborhood, Emmitt resigns himself to the reality that Lindsay may not be home for the night. He opens the driver's side door upon which he has been leaning for the last few hours and sits down. It would be impossible for him to ransack and upturn every single house in this neighborhood. Equally impossible would be for him to single-handedly find his daughter.

In effect, Emmitt recognizes his helplessness. Although he wants to kill for his daughter, there is nothing he can do. His position hasn't changed. In this state, he does something he hasn't done in years. He crosses himself and whispers a prayer.

"In the name of the Father, the Son, and the Holy Spirit," he says. Slowly, he keys the ignition and pulls away from the curb to go home. Emmitt realizes how ridiculous he looks. From a bystander's point of view, he probably looks like he's driving around the neighborhood in his van to score drugs.

In a sense, Emmitt is looking to score. Perhaps an act of petition raised to Heaven would score him some points. Perhaps enough would allow him to cash in for an answered prayer. Emmitt laughs bitterly at this thought. Of course, he doesn't believe that this is the way prayer works. Though he has been away from the church and even failed to go to confession a few years ago when Father Klein invited him, he knows better than to think that prayer is answered according to one's own merit.

Surveying the streets as though Lindsay will somehow magically appear, Emmitt sighs. He drives home, trailing behind him the certainty of disappointment.

Chapter Twenty-Seven

June 23, 2011

Without a word, three months pass, and Lindsay still hasn't returned home. As any distraught parent would do, Emmitt canvases countless neighborhoods with flyers of Lindsay's face. On the weekends, he knocks on doors and talks to anyone that would listen as he explains his daughter's disappearance. During the weekdays, immediately after work, he takes the old van through the neighborhood of Main and New Hampshire. Each day, he drives through the neighborhood, past the boarded-up homes that seem ready to be demolished for green space. And, each day, he makes a stop before coming into the neighborhood at the same convenience store and speaks to the same three young men. Naturally, his regular visits open the way for a relationship of trust, and he gets to know Marco, the leader of the group, and his pals, Andre, and Jordan.

"Hey, Mr. W.," says Marco as he laughs at Emmitt, pulling into the parking lot. That's the usual greeting he gets, and it rarely changes. Andre and Jordan are equally friendly.

"What's the news, Marco?" Emmitt asks.

Marco eyes Andre and Jordan. Emmitt takes this exchange in and recognizes it for what it is. His heart rate quickens. Andre and Jordan shake their heads as they step back.

"Don't worry about them," Marco says. "They've got some reservations. We saw your boy, Troy. He's two blocks up and holed up in one of these houses."

"And my daughter?"

Marco shakes his head. "We didn't see her."

In a quick handshake, Marco slips Emmitt a note, telling him to open it in the car. Once on the road, Emmitt does so and sees an address: 124 New Hampshire Dr. He passes this house once, giving it a quick glance and sees that it is much like the others with peeled paint and broken windows, though absent of the sheets of plywood and spray paint, serving as a warning to keep out. Slowing the van to a stop across the street, Emmitt takes in the view of 124 New Hampshire from the vantage point of the driver's side mirror while occasionally glancing in his rearview and passenger side mirrors should anyone approach the vehicle from behind. And people do. Neighborhood kids, walking down the street, eye him, and so do some adults.

As he continues to survey the house, he wonders what Troy and Lindsay could be doing in there. He shakes his head, banishing any bad thoughts. He believes Lindsay is in this predicament because she will go with Troy anywhere, even though Emmitt knows there's no way Troy can make this dump before him a home.

Then, a light flashes from the upstairs window. Emmitt turns in his seat to get a look. From the window, a young man glances down and pulls the curtains closed. Then, a scream follows. The voice sounds female. Lindsay. Going on Marco's word, Emmitt exits the van and runs toward the front door. He pushes the door wide open, and out comes Lindsay in a blur. She collides with Emmitt, knocking them both off balance and to the ground.

"Lindsay!" he cheers. He looks at her as she rolls over. "Are you okay?"

Lindsay groans. She rises to her feet, and Emmitt gasps when he sees her face. Her left eye and cheek are swollen. Although she wears make-up, Emmitt notices fading bruises, which leads him to believe this isn't the first time she's been hurt like this.

"Fuck you come from?" someone asks from behind Emmitt. Emmitt gets up and slowly turns. Troy stares down at him from the stoop. Troy tucks something in his pocket.

"Oh, hey, Mr. Wasson, I didn't know it was you," Troy says, forcing a friendly smile.

"Did you do this?" asks Emmitt as he marches up the steps to Troy.

"Hey, man, you got the wrong guy. It was —"

But Emmitt doesn't wait for Troy's answer. He grabs Troy and slams him against the door. Emmitt frisks Troy to find a gun tucked in his pocket.

"Are you gonna shoot her?" he asks angrily.

"Nah, you got it all wrong," replies Troy.

"The fuck I do!" Emmitt launches Troy down the steps, but not before Troy lands a swipe at Emmitt's stomach. Troy's punch hits Emmitt hard as he doubles over and struggles to catch his breath. As Troy recovers from his fall, he crouches by Lindsay.

"You get away from her," Emmitt says between breaths.

"Please," pleads Troy. "I told you, it wasn't —"

Emmitt grabs hold of Troy, pulls him toward himself, and punches him right in the face, sending him to the pavement with a thud. With Troy apparently out, Emmitt goes to Lindsay and checks her pulse. Feeling that it is strong, he gets up and grabs his phone to dial 911.

As Emmitt waits next to Lindsay, her eyes flutter open.

"Daddy, what are you doing here?" she asks weakly.

"I've found you, kiddo," Emmitt says. He smiles and gently strokes her other cheek. "You're safe now. You don't have to worry about Troy anymore."

"What do you mean?" Lindsay rises slowly. "Where is he?" When Lindsay's gaze lands on Troy unconscious, she lets out a blood-curdling scream. "Oh, God! Troy!"

"Lindsay, you're —"

"What happened to him?" Lindsay looks up at Emmitt. "Did they do this to him?"

"What are you talking about?"

"These guys hit me." Lindsay touches her face on one of the spots she used make-up to cover. "They must have run. Did you see them?"

Emmitt frowns. "No, I —"

Sirens blare, and lights flash as Emmitt stands, looking over his daughter and kneeling beside Troy. Blood trickles down his nose and onto his cheek. From where he is standing, Emmitt thinks Troy will be okay. At the most, the young man may have a concussion. Paramedics rush onto the scene, pulling Troy onto a stretcher, away from Emmitt and Lindsay. Then, the police arrive with questions.

During questioning, Emmitt tells his side of the story. He believes Troy is beating Lindsay, so he intervenes to save her. Yet only a few hours pass as Emmitt sits by Lindsay in Troy's hospital room, sharing a bittersweet family reunion in which he confesses to her. Better to hear it first from him than from someone else, he reasons. Not surprisingly, she banishes him from the room and finds her own way home sometime late at night.

* * *

"He's gonna press charges, you know," Lindsay says when she arrives home.

"Well, hello, to you, too," says Emmitt as he grits his

teeth. "Can we not talk about Troy right now? He's not even awake."

"Yeah, well, when he does wake up, you'll see." Lindsay leans closer. "Why'd you do it?"

"I was protecting you, Lindsay. Can't you see that?"

"He was protecting me. You've always hated Troy."

"That's not true. Somewhere he went wrong."

"When? Maybe if you'd met him halfway. He tried so hard to get you to like him."

"I didn't see —"

"No, Dad, you didn't. You were too busy *not* being my Dad."

"Lindsay, I— "

"I'm leaving. Don't talk to me."

With a slam of the door, the floodwaters of guilt rush over Emmitt, and his daughter is gone again.

CHAPTER TWENTY-EIGHT

June 27, 2011

Alone in the dark with a bottle of whiskey, Emmitt sits in the house next to the home phone. The first night, Frank Burgess came by to check on him. He didn't stay long, as Emmitt didn't speak. Aside from the occasional delivery person that visits Emmitt's doorstep, Emmitt is a recluse — a man of solitary confinement within the prison of his own home. The blinds are shut as he wallows in darkness. A knock on the door causes him to rise from his seat and open the door.

Two officers stand at the door. Behind them are two more officers, and each one stands with their hands resting on the hilt of their weapons. Emmitt raises his hands.

"Mr. Wasson, you're under arrest for assault and battery," says the officer.

Chapter Twenty-Nine

December 21, 2011

"We've caught him," Frank Burgess says.

Emmitt stares at him. Through the glare of the plexiglass, he reads the grim expression on Frank's face. Three months ago, Frank came to tell him Lindsay had gone missing again. With Frank as Lindsay's godfather, Emmitt feels like Frank should have more control over her, but Frank feels differently.

Sometimes, you gotta let them go.

Frank has told Emmitt that before, but now it makes more sense. Although Emmitt is upset with Frank, he lets his emotions pass.

"Have you found Lindsay?" Emmitt asks.

A pregnant pause. Emmitt waits with dread and anticipation as his heart thumps in his chest, fearing the worst, though anticipating some middle ground between the worst and the best. Perhaps she was high when the Sheriff's department caught Troy.

"We found her," Frank says. "Troy crashed the car and ditched her. Then, he ditched the heroin. We found it.

Then, we found —"

"Lindsay." Emmitt blinks twice. "What the fuck? Was she conscious?"

Frank shakes his head. "We rushed her to the hospital. An OD. But she's in recovery. Daniella's with her right now."

"I just wish—"

"What? Do you want to go back in time, so you can do things differently?" Frank leans in. "There's nothing you could have done differently. She made her own choices. The best we can do now is to help her through it."

"It didn't work last time. With me in jail and the grudge I'm sure she carries, how's it going to work this time?"

"I don't know, Emmitt. The best we can do is what we've done in the past. Be there for her. A three month's reprieve in recovery is better than nothing."

Emmitt nods. "There's a board hearing coming up. Maybe you could speak on my behalf. It would be your word as law enforcement, you know?"

"Anything you want, Emmitt," Frank says. "If it were me, the prick would have gotten much worse for dragging Lindsay into this world. But, as you know, I wouldn't say that at all."

CHAPTER THIRTY

January 28, 2012

Out in seven. Not bad, Emmitt thinks.

Emmitt squints as the early morning sun casts a glare over the snowy fields just beyond the prison parking lot. He breathes in the crisp, cold morning air. Though he has spent the last month, worrying about Lindsay's recovery, the snow that wisps through the January breeze puts him at ease. Frank has told Emmitt that Lindsay has recovered in his absence, so now Emmitt plans to start fresh. Fresh, like the first footprint that makes its mark in newly fallen snow on a cold, clear morning.

Or anything but, Emmitt thinks to himself as Frank Burgess pulls up in a patrol vehicle.

"Give ya a ride," Frank says. "Lindsay's home. She was quiet this morning."

Emmitt accepts Frank's offer as the officer drops him off home. As they pull into the neighborhood, Emmitt can tell his friends, Daniella and Frank, have maintained the place while he's been gone. His driveway is clear from snow. Not to mention, a fresh linen scent wafts through the air when Emmitt enters the house. Although the scent does a decent job of masking the staleness of the house, Emmitt coughs anyway. He realizes he needs to dust more.

"Lindsay, I'm back!" he shouts. "Where are you?"

"In here, Dad," she calls from the kitchen. "Uncle Frank and Aunt Daniella said they'd be over in fifteen minutes."

"I guess they want to give us time to talk."

Lindsay turns to him and nods. "Yeah, I guess so." She turns her back to him and begins to chop some food.

"What're you putting together?" Emmitt asks. He reaches around her and snatches a carrot, the first thing within his reach, in an attempt to let his daughter know with just a quick brush that she is still his little girl.

"Dad!" Lindsay smacks his hand.

Emmitt snags a carrot and takes a bite. "What?"

An uncomfortable silence lays heavy in the air between Emmitt and Lindsay. Even the crunch of Emmitt's carrot ceases as he looks into his daughter's eyes. They are blue but hurting. Emmitt can see that the little girl he once knew is gone. Before him is his daughter, who has felt the sting of drug addiction; a sting penetrating far deeper than his own devastating bout with addiction. Though she is clear for the moment, a mere suggestion and she could easily turn back and be lost forever.

"I'm not letting you go," Emmitt says as he pulls Lindsay into an embrace. She resists at first but gives in only slightly.

"We should probably talk," Emmitt says and steps away from Lindsay.

"You don't have to bullshit me," Lindsay says bluntly. "I know Troy abandoned me. Whatever."

"I've got you," Emmitt says. "We can do this together."

* * *

And they do. Emmitt insists that Lindsay goes back to high school. Though it takes all of the school days, nights, and weekends for her to catch up, Emmitt sees her walk the stage at the end of the school year, and he beams with pride.

In the interim, the time between Lindsay going back to school and finishing, Emmitt struggles to find work. With a felony on his record, he can no longer return to his security position. However, he does return to his old job at the factory, bottling sodas on the day shift. And together, Emmitt and Lindsay fall into a routine. He drops her off, goes to work, and picks her up after school. On Friday nights, the two have dinner with Frank and Daniella, and, by all appearances, they appear to be a healthy family. Over dinner, Emmitt occasionally catches the forlorn gaze of his daughter, who flashes him a half-hearted smile and turns away to scrutinize some distant scene somewhere far beyond the landscape of a pristine neighborhood.

"Hey," Emmitt says as he reaches over the table and takes her hand. "What's on your mind?"

"Nothing," Lindsay says. "Just got a big test tomorrow."

Over the years, Emmitt has learned that it is never just a big test, another major assignment, or even a lot of homework. So, he presses her, refusing to give up.

"I want to help, Lindsay. I know there is more to it than school. Is it Troy?"

Lindsay nods. "I wrote to him."

Though the need to explain, to solve the problem, to convince his daughter never to write to him again courses through his veins as his heart races, Emmitt breathes in this news and waits.

"He didn't respond," Lindsay continues. "He could be hurt. Or worse. I...we should see him."

"No, I don't think we should. Think about —"

"My future." Lindsay snorts. "Is that what you were

going to say? I think about it all the time. He's not..."
Tears well up in her eyes. "Excuse me." Lindsay leaves
the table, and her unfinished meal goes cold.

Emmitt sits alone at the table. He cringes at the
thought that Troy could easily be back in Lindsay's life.
Or maybe something could happen where he doesn't get
out. They could easily lose a young good-looking guy
like him in the prison system. Perhaps some mishap
with the paperwork could occur. Or perhaps he could
get additional time for lashing out at some inmates.

Emmitt shakes his head as he can't believe he is
wishing ill will on Troy. No man, he reminds himself,
regardless of how far he has gone, is beyond
redemption. God, it's been a long time since he has
thought about redemption, especially within his
Catholic faith. He wonders if his life or Lindsay's life
would be any different if he had been more faithful.

Emmitt leaves the half-finished food and dirty dishes
on the table and follows Lindsay upstairs. He
approaches the darkness within her room and enters the
open doorway to find her lying asleep, face buried in her
pillow.

He sits on the bed, which stirs Lindsay awake.

"Daddy, is that you?" she asks.

"Yup," says Emmitt with a smile. He appreciates how
Lindsay, despite everything she has been through, has
never completely abandoned the practice of calling him
this.

"I'm here," Emmitt says. He leans over and kisses her
on her cheek. "I'll be here for you...and Troy if needed."

Chapter Thirty-One

August 16, 2014

The prison looms over Emmitt, but Lindsay seated in the passenger seat beside him, doesn't seem to notice. She is giddy, like a freshman girl, awaiting the arrival of her date to senior prom. Ironic, since Lindsay has never been to prom due to her circumstances: drugs and her infatuation with Troy. A half smile, formed neither of joy nor of nostalgia but of regret, forms on Emmitt's face as he thinks of his daughter, preparing for a date she never had and fussing over the smallest of details—the stray lock of hair that just can't stay behind her ear, or the make-up that needs to be applied smoothly and evenly so as to hide the teenage blemish of an acne scar still healing over from a recently popped pimple. Of course, Maggie would have handled all of this if she had not died too soon. And he wonders if she would have had the chance if she had lived to see Lindsay into her teenage years. Emmitt sighs deeply and exhales the years of time lost.

"Are you okay, Dad?" Lindsay asks.

"Yeah," he says with a sigh. "Just thinking about your

mother." His reply is a half-truth. The half he didn't tell is too ugly for Emmitt to say aloud. He's unwilling to tell Lindsay none of this — the drugs, Troy, Emmitt's abandonment as a father — would have happened had Maggie still been around.

"That's funny," Lindsay says softly. "I was just thinking about her, too. After all this time, I still miss her."

Emmitt doesn't reply. Instead, he looks at the gate out of which Troy would soon be exiting to enjoy his freedom. Troy's father, Leo Andreadis, should have been here waiting for Troy. But this morning, Emmitt finds Leo in another drunken state. Some people just never truly change, Emmitt realizes as his eyes focus on his daughter.

"Lindsay, I'm not going to lie," Emmitt says. "I'm worried about Troy getting out. About what that might do to you. It's easy to be reformed when you're on the inside to be reformed. I've been there with prison. Then with rehab. So, have you. What's going to keep Troy from just returning to what he left?"

"He's got us, Dad. All of us. You, me, Frank and Daniella. And God."

"And God," Emmitt repeats, though his voice betrays uncertainty. Is it possible that an infinite God could keep them all moving forward toward full recovery? For Emmitt, he holds his doubts.

"He's coming, Daddy. Look!" Lindsay hops out of the van and leaves the door open as she runs to Troy, who is just stepping up to the gate and waiting for the guard to unleash him to freedom.

And there he is, Emmitt observes. Troy's shit face grin perfectly complimenting his tall thin frame and permanently tanned skin.

"Thank you so much, Mr. Wasson," Troy says as he leans into the passenger side and glances inside. "Where's my pop?"

"He couldn't make it, but he says he'll see you at

home."

"He must be drunk again." Troy sucks his teeth.

Emmitt nods. "Get in."

There's no point pretending some other reality is in play. Troy slides into the rear passenger seat. Lindsay shuts the front passenger door and slides next to him. Emmitt glances in the rearview mirror only to see the two, almost perfect strangers to him, ogling each other. Lindsay leans against Troy. Emmitt keys the ignition, backs up, and peels out of the parking lot without waiting to hear the resounding click of two seatbelts that would indicate his precious cargo, excluding Troy, is safely secured in the back seat.

CHAPTER THIRTY-TWO

November 2, 2014

As months pass, Emmitt mentally marks each day Troy makes it into work. After all, it is not just Troy whose days are measured one tick at a time. Emmitt has used the tally system for Lindsay and himself over the years.

Emmitt flips open the cell phone as he sits with Frank on the Burgess's front porch.

"Let it be, Emmitt," Frank says. "You only need to worry about yourself."

"But she said she'd be home tonight," says Emmitt. "He promised the same."

"How long since your last temptation?" Frank asks.

"Maybe sixteen years, give or take. But what does that have to do with anything?"

"Nothing. Maybe everything. I'm not sure. Maybe the point I'm making is that you can only control yourself and the way you interact with what is happening around you. For all you know, they could be rounding that corner right now." Frank points. "That light just ahead could be theirs."

Emmitt stands and leans over the railing and watches

as a car passes by. Not Troy's. He checks the phone again, not that he is expecting the phone to suddenly ring or buzz for a text message. That would be great, but at nearly midnight and with his need to turn in for the evening, he finds Lindsay's number on speed dial and holds the phone to his ear, and listens. There is no answer as the phone rings several times before cutting out. Emmitt stuffs it into his pocket and plops down on the wicker chair.

"She should've been home over two hours ago," Emmitt says. "That's what she promised."

"I'm sure she's fine," Frank says.

But Emmitt detects the doubt in his friend's voice. With over thirty years with the Sheriff's department and with most of those years as Sheriff, Frank knows better. But Emmitt doesn't contest. He simply waves.

"I guess I'll head in for the night," he says. "I'll let you know if I need anything."

* * *

Sometime around two in the morning, Emmitt's phone rings. He reaches for it as the phone vibrates across the nightstand and comes dangerously close to falling. Before the phone drops, Emmitt clasps it in his hand and answers the call from the unknown number.

"Hello," he says. "Who's this?"

"Daddy," Lindsay cries. "Come get me. I'm… I don't think I'm going to make it."

"I'll be right there." Emmitt wipes a clammy hand on his jeans. "Where are you?"

"I'm not sure… Main Street, I think. It looks the same from the last time you were here."

"I'll be there. Is Troy with you?"

"No, I don't know where he is!"

Over the phone, Emmitt hears the peel of tires and sirens blaring in the distance.

"Get inside. Lock the doors. I'll call you when I'm

close."

After throwing on some sweatpants and yesterday's socks, Emmitt stuffs his feet into a pair of work boots and clumps quickly to the door. By the door rests a bat. This he grabs in the event some force is needed, though he leaves behind his handgun because he doesn't trust himself not to use it should it come to that. Forgetting about Frank, Emmitt hops into the Pinto he purchased a few years ago, keys the ignition, and takes off, buckling his seatbelt only when he is well on his way down the road. As he drives, he imagines that Troy has gotten himself back into the old life he claimed to have left behind. Perhaps some thug from that life roped Troy back into. Or, more likely, Troy never left this life behind and only put on an act for the parole board, Lindsay, and more specifically, Emmitt that he might drop his guard. Little does Troy know that Emmitt never dropped his guard. How could he trust him, especially when it comes to his daughter's safety?

The phone beside him rings. Emmitt grabs it.

"Yeah, I'm on my way," says Emmitt. "I should be there in twenty."

"Emmitt, it's me," Frank says. "Where you headed? I heard you leave."

"Shit, I'm sorry, Frank. I thought you were Lindsay. She called and wants me to pick her up. It sounded serious. Like she was in some kind of trouble."

"Where is it? I can back you up."

Emmitt relays the location to Frank, hangs up the phone, and puts pressure on the gas pedal.

Rounding the dark corner of Main Street, Emmitt calls Lindsay on her phone. There's no answer. It is not until he is a block away from the house that he sees the problem. A group of three men surrounds a smaller-framed person, possibly a female and more likely Lindsay. As they circle her, their intentions, while they remain ambiguous to Emmitt, could only mean to do her harm. Emmitt punches the gas, and as he does, he catches the blue and red flash of sirens in his mirrors. He hits the breaks and brings the truck to a screeching halt beside the group, and jumps out of the truck, swinging the bat wildly toward one man, then another, protecting the victim from whatever intentions they had. The men run away just as the cruiser stops.

"You alright, Emmitt?" Franks says as he gets out.

"Yeah, I'm good," says Emmitt as he catches his breath. "These punks. I don't know what they wanted with Lindsay, but —"

"Who's Lindsay?" the girl asks.

Emmitt spins around and sees the brown eyes of a woman, staring back at him. She is young, though he can tell drug use is aging her.

"I'm sorry," says Emmitt hastily. "I thought you were my daughter."

"Well, thanks anyway," she says. Then she looks at Frank. "Can I go, officer? Do you need a statement?"

"No," says Frank. "You're free to go." Frank shakes his head as the girl runs off. Then, he looks to Emmitt. "So, I take it you didn't find her?"

Emmitt shakes his head, barely believing that he possibly risked his own life for this stranger. Not to mention that Lindsay could easily have been just like this woman had she not gotten the treatment she needed. Even worse though, she still could be exactly like this woman if she continues to spend time down here.

"Daddy," Lindsay calls.

Emmitt spins in her direction and sees her running across the street. Relief and exhaustion flood over him, and he sits on the curb.

"That was incredible," she says as she reaches out to hug him.

When she wraps her arms around him, Emmitt recoils and pushes her away as he stands.

"That could have been you!" he shouts. "What are you thinking, staying down here?"

Tears well up in her pale, blue eyes. She averts her gaze and stares at the ground.

"Well, here's what I think," Frank says, stepping between Emmitt and Lindsay. "Why don't you two try to talk tomorrow? I'll drive Lindsay home in my patrol car."

"Yeah," Emmitt says in a voice just above a whisper. "That's probably better." Then, he steps away and heads to the open door of his truck. Just before stepping into the driver's seat, he sees Lindsay open the passenger seat of the patrol car. He and his daughter stand there, looking at each other without saying a word. Emmitt is the first to turn away. He slams the door behind him, which causes some loose parts of the truck to rattle.

The drive home seems long. Emmitt doesn't drive home with the same urgency he drove into the city. No, he is prolonging the inevitable conversation he must have with Lindsay, and he can only come back to the same cause — Troy. In fact, he wouldn't be surprised if Troy is somehow related to the incident with the woman involved with the three men from earlier. Of course, he probably only delayed whatever danger she was in anyway, and this woman, though she wasn't Lindsay, might as well have been. Maybe Emmitt was fighting for this woman in lieu of the father she never had.

But either way, something brought Lindsay to this point, and Emmitt intends to find out for her sake and for his own. But not tonight. Tonight, she will be at Frank and Daniella's house. Tonight, Emmitt will try to get some sleep, and sometime the following afternoon, after he gets off work, he will have the talk with Lindsay. Perhaps time with the Burgesses will have prepared her for this conversation.

* * *

Emmitt and Lindsay, a father and his adult daughter, sit on the back porch in silence. Emmitt has been off work, and he still wears his work clothes now. He has been sitting here with Lindsay for nearly two hours. Two, untouched glasses of lemonade sit between them. The condensation on the glasses has since dried. The ice cubes have dissolved. Emmitt knows the drinks are watery by now, but he still reaches for his glass. Lindsay does the same. As he sips, he makes a face and sets down the glass of what he confirms as bitter, watered down lemonade.

"I guess I'll go first," Emmitt says. "You called. What happened?"

"I don't know," Lindsay says as she looks at the glass she is rotating clockwise in her hand. "One moment, Troy was there. The next, he yelled for help. I went out. I didn't see him."

Emmitt nods and withholds judgement despite the smell of bullshit. "And you didn't hear from him today?"

Lindsay shakes her head. "I think he's in trouble."

"Is it his past life catching up to him? Or is this new?"

She shrugs. "Just some pot. That's all."

Refraining from rehashing worn out lectures, Emmitt takes another bitter sip of lemonade. He knows there's more to Lindsay's story, so he waits.

"But I don't think that's it," Lindsay continues. "There has to be more to it. When Emmitt dealt with these guys last time —"

"What do you mean by last time?" asks Emmitt. He narrows his eyes.

"I mean..." Lindsay pauses. "They came looking for some money from him last time. Then, this time. I know he didn't have any, but he took them outside. That's when I heard them fighting. Then they were gone. You don't think..."

"I don't know, Lindsay." Emmitt says. "Let's hope for the best. He'll return. I have no doubt about that."

"Oh, I hope you're right, Daddy." Lindsay stands and bends over to embrace Emmitt, who remains in his seat.

"I'm gonna get some sleep, okay?"

Lindsay heads into the house while Emmitt remains outside. He still ponders the truthfulness of the statements he made to his daughter. Though his truth and wishes for Troy may differ entirely from his daughter's own unfinished thoughts, Emmitt would certainly not wish the death of anyone. Rather, the best-case scenario would be that Troy realizes the danger he is putting Lindsay in and stays away. Or, if he does return, it'll be in handcuffs, caught once again for doing something illegal. After all, whatever he is doing, it is probably a violation of his parole, which would be too bad, especially since, up to this point, Troy had worked so hard to put on such a convincing show of reform for nearly everyone in town to see.

Chapter Thirty-Three

October 21, 2016

Careening through a neighborhood littered with trash, Emmitt jostles in the driver's seat of a clanking white pickup patched with black paint. He wears a camouflage ball cap stuffed upon his greying head, and his face sports the stubble of a man who has neglected, rather than chosen, not to shave for a few days.

He squints at the rearview mirror and out the side windows until he spots his turn, a tight alleyway half a block ahead. Over time, Emmitt uses this turn as a shortcut to Troy's dumpy house, where Lindsay now lives. As he turns into the alleyway, his truck tires squeal just as Emmitt's phone, which sits in the empty passenger seat, rings.

Glancing quickly at the caller ID, he sees Lindsay's name flash on the screen.

"I'm on my way," Emmitt mutters. He pushes the gas pedal, and the truck careens forward, causing the bed to fishtail and scatter a couple of grey trash cans and their contents onto a brown patch of backyard lawn.

Pumping the brakes as he rounds a left turn out the

alley, Emmitt barely slows down. It was his daughter's call which interrupted his hunting trip with Frank. She has left a voicemail, sounding scared.

"Daddy, please come get me. Troy hurt me badly. I'm scared, and...I'm ready to go home."

The message from Lindsay has ended. Emmitt isn't sure when he felt the change, but he blacks out. His buddy Frank has been mentioning he could ride with him to get Lindsay, but all Emmitt remembers is mechanically walking to his truck, starting the ignition, and letting Frank tap the hood to show the car is good to go. Somewhere in the cab of the truck, Emmitt has a hunting rifle. Tonight, he might need it.

The phone beside him rings again as Emmitt brings the truck, squealing around another corner. His rifle, loosely latched on the mount inside of the cab, rattles and crashes to the rusty floor beside a box of ammunition and a small wooden baseball bat, the barrel of which is darkly discolored. The phone continues to ring.

"Shit," he yells just as he spots his daughter, darting out of Troy's row home. The façade of the house looms behind her in crumbling decay as she slows to a frantic pace while holding the phone to her ear. The phone's receiving end rings incessantly within the truck. As Emmitt reaches toward the phone, Lindsay turns, spots the truck, and waves. As she does, Troy, tan with tattoos up and down his bare arms, steps out of the house and off the stoop. His gait is steady yet menacing as he closes the space between himself and Lindsay. She turns. Though lanky, his height dominates over her petite frame. She backs away.

Seeing this, Emmitt slams on his brakes and opens the door while grabbing the bat from the floor. He leaps out of the car, past his daughter, and shoves Troy to the ground, causing him to slide and scrape his back against gravel and shards of loose concrete. Emmitt steps toward Troy and swings the bat down, aiming toward his face, but he misses. Troy rolls over, hops off the ground, and dashes down the street.

Lindsay steps toward her father, who turns to see his little girl beneath the make-up and three tattoos, which mark her pale skin on her arm, her shoulder, and her neck. Her face is appallingly thin, and he notices a red welt below her eye, which is barely visible beneath hastily applied makeup and mascara. He looks into her eyes, the whites of which are marred by tiny red veins. Stepping toward her, he reaches with his free hand in an open gesture to touch her face. She circumvents his attempt at affection by twisting away. He drops his hand.

"Get a change of clothing," he says. "Nothing more."

She nods, walks toward the house, then breaks into a run and passes into the darkness beyond the entryway. Alone on the stoop, Emmitt hears the rapid creaking of each step as she ascends to the second floor of the house. Faltering in a moment's preparation on the stoop, Emmitt follows his daughter into the shadowy interior of the house. Immediately, the smell of rotting wood, stale urine, and body odor, overwhelms his senses, forcing him to step back into the fresh air. He inhales and exhales several times as he pulls a handkerchief from his back pocket and holds it over his nose.

In this way, he re-enters the house and follows Lindsay upstairs. Upon reaching the doorway to her bedroom, he removes the handkerchief from his mouth and chokes again on the stench. He enters her room and finds her, sitting at the edge of her bed and holding a plastic grocery bag filled with a wad of clothing.

"Dump it out," Emmitt demands.

She looks at her father. Her blue eyes glisten with tears that threaten to wash away the eyeliner and the make-up caked over bumps and blemishes on what was once clear and perfect skin. Emmitt drops his eyes and sees the inside of her arms, one of which contains needle marks no more than a few days old. Lindsay follows her father's eyes.

"I've quit," she whispers.

"Dump it out, or I walk away now."

A dark tear rolls down her cheek as she spills the contents of the bag onto the floor and returns his gaze with an aqueous stare.

Emmitt crosses his arms as he stares at the pile of clothes on the floor. "Shake and fold each item and put them back one-by-one."

Lindsay bites her lip and furrows her brow as she kneels on the floor to pick up each crumpled item. With care, she shakes each article of clothing and neatly folds them afterwards. When she picks up her jeans, she glances at her father then back at the jeans in her hands. She stands, holds the jeans by the waist, and gives them a violent shake before folding them in half.

"What's in the right pocket?" Emmitt asks.

"Nothing," Lindsay whispers.

"Hold the jeans from the bottom and give them a shake."

As she does so, a needle and a small plastic bag falls to the floor next to her feet. She's wearing pink flip-flops, and her toes look as though they were recently manicured. Though the nail polish on her big toe is smeared, Emmitt releases the tension in his jaw.

"I'm glad you're still taking care of some of your appearances," he says hoarsely.

"Yeah," Lindsay says as she stares at the floor, biting her bottom lip.

Emmitt clears his throat. "Anything else in your jeans?"

Lindsay pulls the inside of the pockets out. "That's it."

Emmitt nods, and Lindsay folds the jeans and places them on top of the other items in the bag.

"Now, flush it away," Emmitt says as he gestures toward the floor where the plastic bag had remained.

Lindsay shifts her feet and knocks the bag away. In protest, she begins, "But, I —"

Emmitt pivots toward the door with disinterest.

"Wait." Lindsay stoops to the floor and picks up the bag and the needle. Holding these two items in her hand, she walks past her father, who follows her to the dingy, dimly lit bathroom where she lifts the toilet lid, and stops when she hears a crash from the first floor. The noise is followed by the rapid stomping down the steps. Emmitt turns to face the ruckus, and he's met by Troy.

"Hey!" Troy shouts. "That's my fuckin' livelihood you're about to flush!" His eyes grow wide as Emmitt lifts the bat and prepares to swing. "C'mon, man." Troy backs away and down the steps. "A guy's gotta eat."

"And get high," Emmitt adds. "And get my daughter high." He eyes Troy, who is beginning to make his way back up the steps. Emmitt swings, but misses as Troy ducks, and then retreats. Emmitt makes to chase, but from behind him, Lindsay whimpers.

"Daddy, no!" she yells. "Please, don't make me do this." He turns around and sees that she is still by the toilet, holding the bag and the needle.

"Drop it," Emmitt says.

Lindsay stomps her foot and pouts, like a child. For a moment, her posture reminds Emmitt of long ago when, as a little girl, she demanded ice cream before her bedtime. He stands there, silent, cold, and firm. She shifts her feet, crosses her arms, then sniffs and wipes a wet, dark smudge from her cheek, all while looking beyond her father.

"You can have the bitch!" Troy yells from downstairs by the door, which immediately slams shut.

"I'm gonna come back when he apologizes," Lindsay says as she finally looks into Emmitt's eyes.

"Fine," Emmitt says, as he does an about-face and walks toward the landing.

"Wait, no!" Lindsay shouts as Emmitt leaves. "Don't go!" She starts sobbing, which causes Emmitt to stop and turn toward her. She is on her knees, clutching the bag and needle. Her sobbing subsides as she rocks herself and leans against the toilet.

"Lindsay," he says at last. "I love you, but it's me or that." He places his hand on his chest. "Me or Troy."

She blinks slowly, frozen and seemingly incapable of a decision. Emmitt slumps his shoulders and begins a slow, creaky descent toward the front door, which he discovers is still open. A shadow lurks by the door, but quickly disappears. From outside, a car door slams. From inside and upstairs, Emmitt hears the flush of the toilet. Moments later, Lindsay descends the staircase. He casts his gaze upon his daughter, who is standing small amidst the shadows of the second-floor landing. She bows her head and holds her bag of clothes.

"It's done," she says without looking at him. "I'm ready."

Slowly, he continues his descent toward the front door until he hears his daughter's feet, matching in time and rhythm with his several steps behind him. Once outside, he heads to his truck and smiles to see that Troy is nowhere in sight. When he tosses the bat on the floor of the truck, it lands with a clank next to the box of ammunition still lying on the floor. At this moment, Emmitt remembers his gun had crashed to the floor. Now, it is missing.

From behind him, Emmitt hears the rapid patter of footsteps on concrete. Lindsay screams. Then, he hears the familiar *click* and *bang* of his rifle. Searing, sudden pain rips into his back.

Emmitt falls to the ground. He rolls onto his back and lifts his head to catch a glimpse of the house. Troy stands there, and Lindsay is next to him. From a distance, she appears wide-eyed. The mascara she wears has completely streaked down her face from the tears. One of her hands covers her mouth, and the other hand is at her side, slack and holding her father's hunting rifle, which slips and lands on a patch of brown, dead grass next to the stoop.

Lindsay screams and runs to him. She kneels by his

side, and her face is above his. She is crying, and between sobs and breaths, sound but no decipherable words come out of her mouth. Emmitt closes his eyes. He tries to focus his attention on his daughter's cries. The sound of sirens and horns draws nearer as he slips in and out of consciousness.

"Hold on, Daddy!" she cries. "I'm sorry. Just hold on." Sirens blare louder as the red and blue lights flash. Doors open and slam of what Emmitt believes are cop cars. Someone rips Lindsay away from his side, and her cries go abruptly silent with the slam of another door. Somewhere between darkness and light, consciousness and unconsciousness, Emmitt hears Frank's voice amidst the paramedics and uniformed officers on the scene.

"What the fuck happened, boys?" asks Frank.

"Looks like a domestic," another officer says.

Frank's face appears over Emmitt.

"Shit, Emmitt," he huffs. "Look what you've gone and done this time."

Emmitt answers Frank with a grunt, then he closes his eyes and embraces the peaceful silence of unconsciousness.

Chapter Thirty-Four

October 26, 2016

Regaining consciousness to the sound of an incessant beeping, Emmitt forces his eyes open. As he sits up, the darkness disorients him at first as he tries to make sense of his surroundings. Save for a pale green glow behind him and the stream of light coming from the door, Emmitt would have a hard time adjusting, especially since he has no recollection of arriving here. He tries to rise from his bed to stand when his efforts to do so are stymied by a sudden stabbing pain in his back.

"God!" he cries. "Shit, that hurts!"

As the door opens, the crack of light widens until it is eclipsed by a woman. She approaches him and places her hand on his chest and begins to count.

"Your vitals are good," the nurse says as she checks his pulse and then stuffs a thermometer in his mouth. "How you feeling today?"

"Okay, I guess," he mumbles with the thermometer in his mouth. "How long have I been here?"

"A couple days. You received a gunshot. The doctor will be here sometime in the morning. In the meantime, get some rest. You'll have visitors in the morning. Ring if you need me."

As he lies back down, Emmitt thinks about the events, leading up to this moment, where he is in a hospital with a gunshot wound. Somehow, Lindsay has gotten away from him and entrenched herself in Troy's world. Even worse, she's in a world of addiction that has taken hold of her, dragging her further from her loved ones. Because of her addiction, Emmitt suspects that Lindsay wouldn't be able to tell who her loved ones are because she has been blinded by drugs. What a normal person would perceive as corrective, but loving action would appear to an addict to be an act of vindictiveness meant to punish rather than help a person. Emmitt knew this all too well for himself and meant only to keep from losing Lindsay.

As Emmitt struggles to sleep, within him, despair and hope wage war. Although Lindsay is responsible for her own decisions, Emmitt knows he is responsible for her upbringing that influences her decision making. Whether he could have been more or less strict and whether his actions in some way had an impact on his poor choices are decisions he must accept. One thing Emmitt can do as a parent is hope. He can hope that Lindsay will overcome the shit and vomit of his poor choices and be restored to new life, nevermore to return.

This, Emmitt realizes, can only be accomplished through prayer to a God who waits with longing by a window, day after day until the prodigal returns, battered, bruised, and ragged. And as Emmitt finally drifts off to sleep with the image of his daughter, tears streaming from bloodshot eyes and his own rifle hanging limp from her own hands, he whispers a prayer that she would come back to him. That she would return, and he would embrace and clothe her with his love.

The following morning, Emmitt awakens to find Frank standing over him and Daniella seated in the corner.

"Well, look who's decided to return to the land of the living," Frank says. "How you doing?"

"Sore as shit," says Emmitt as he winces. "How's Lindsay?"

"She's in prison," Daniella whispers as she bows her head.

Emmitt blinks twice. "Prison, but how? What did she —"

"She shot you," Frank interjects.

"What? No, she couldn't have. It was Troy!" The beeping on Emmitt's monitor increases while Frank raises his hand.

"Calm down, Emmitt," he says. "Troy had your rifle, but she grabbed it from him. He tried to wrestle it from her. She shot you."

On the pinnacle between cold stone silence and the hot mess of wailing, Emmitt lays in bed, growing numb as the realization of his daughter's actions against him and the apparent attempts on Troy's part to circumvent this action cuts deep into his heart. Emmitt weeps a silent flood of tears.

"I'm sorry, Emmitt," Frank says as he sits on the edge of the bed. "It came as a shock to us both. If it means anything at all, Troy is in prison, too."

Emmitt nods. "Is she getting treatment?"

"Yes," says Daniella as she stands. "I'm sponsoring Lindsay through her program."

"I'd like to see her," Emmitt says.

"I think she'll want to see you," says Daniella. "But I'm not sure she's quite ready for that. Get your rest, Emmitt. There'll be time over the next year."

Emmitt smiles weakly as his friends get up to leave. In the hospital bed, he's left alone with his thoughts. He feels physical pain from trying to stand and emotional pain from Lindsay's actions. Still, he loves his daughter, and he is glad she's getting the help she needs. With at least one reassuring thought, he drifts to sleep.

CHAPTER THIRTY-FIVE

Months pass, and the physical wounds heal until a scar remains. Though invisible when Emmitt sees himself bare chested in the mirror, he has only to turn and look over his shoulder in the mirror to see that scar. Once a hole, with a dark, purple wound closed over with stitches, it's now a divot of white, smooth skin that serves as a reminder, as if he needed one, of what Lindsay did to him. It doesn't matter now. He chose to forgive her. He didn't need the counsel of Father Klein, Dr. Phillips, or even two of his closest friends to come to this decision. As he learned long ago, the best choice is always forgiveness without any conditions set up in which the opportunity for another betrayal of trust can occur.

There is a knock at the front door of the house, and Emmitt ceases to look at his back in the mirror. He quickly grabs the blue button up, hanging from the bathroom hook, and puts it on as he walks to the front of the house while making sure he tucks in his shirt. There is another knock, and he opens the door.

"It looks like you're about ready," Frank says. Behind him is Daniella. Though Emmitt has insisted that they need not accompany him on his visit to Lindsay, the couple wanted to go. Daniella reminds Emmitt that she is Lindsay's sponsor, so she should be there anyway.

Grabbing his coat, Emmitt follows Frank and Daniella into a crisp January morning. As he breathes in the cold air, damp with moisture and the scent of snow, Emmitt smiles. Just as the sudden burst of cold air heightens the senses, Emmitt feels the same sensation as he prepares to visit Lindsay from prison. He has hope for the life that waits for her on the outside of those walls.

It is with nervousness that Emmitt enters the minimum-security prison designed specifically to rehabilitate addicts who committed crimes while under the influence of their drug of choice. Though the facility clearly bears the marks of prison — multiple gates that buzz before they open to enter, a quick pat down, walkthrough of a metal detector, and a check of the identification — he is surprised at the warmth of the place. He is especially surprised when he is seated in a room furnished with a comfortable sofa set and a coffee table. If not for the thick metal door complete with its thick tempered glass, the room could easily be mistaken for a living room of somebody's house. The door to this room remains open as Emmitt, along with Frank and Daniella, sit and listen to the buzzes and echoes common to the halls of nearly every prison.

Following a guard, Lindsay enters the room. Though her face still retains the paleness of a recovering addict, her blue eyes are radiant and clear. She looks to Daniella, Frank, and then finally Emmitt. He takes a step forward while Lindsay steps back. The guard, who brought Lindsay in, tells them they have fifteen minutes and exits the room. The door shuts behind him and locks with a click. With no opportunity for retreat, Lindsay stands there, eyes wide and glistening, looking at Emmitt.

Emmitt steps toward Lindsay and embraces her. Heart to heart, father and daughter cry together, expressing simultaneously love, forgiveness, and promise.

Author's Notes

In 2016, when the idea for this book formed, the national opioid overdose epidemic was over 52,000 lethal drug overdoses, over 20,000 overdose deaths related to pain killers, and close to 13,000 overdose deaths related to heroin. As of January 2019, there was an estimation of more than 130 people who die daily from overdosing on opioids. Though the numbers have dropped slightly since 2015, the crisis is still real.

As an educator, it breaks my heart to hear of the death of a former student due to opioid addiction. In so many cases, this death could have been prevented. Yet, in so many other cases, the life of a young person is lost despite the best efforts of friends, family, counselors, and medical professionals.

In writing this story, I didn't want to patronize the reader by offering some easy solution to helping a friend or family member overcome the addiction. Rather, in these pages I tried to present the scenario as it really is: dark. Yet, even in the darkness, there is always a glimmer of hope to hold onto. In that hope, we hold fast to our loved ones, even when they push us away. We fight for them, even when they've given up the fight. And we find them, even when they seem so hopelessly lost. In the end, we desperately hold onto life.

Thanks for Reading

If you like *A Shot at Mercy*, please consider leaving a review! Indie and small press authors can't survive without word-of-mouth referrals from readers like you.

About the Author

Tim grew up in Syracuse, New York. He currently resides in Maryland where he teaches English, Creative Writing, Film, and Theatre on the middle school level. At the insistence of his own students, he began writing seriously in 2014.

He credits his love for story to his mother, who spent countless hours reading to him and his siblings when they were growing up. Growing up, he devoured the literary words of C. S. Lewis, J. R. R. Tolkien, Piers Anthony, and many others. Mysteries, thrillers, and fantasies are among the genre he most frequently reads. When he's not writing, he's reading, teaching, camping, or enjoying a live music concert.

Visit Tim on the Web

www.timothyrbaldwin.com

www.facebook.com/TimothyRBaldwin

www.instagram.com/timothyrbaldwin